DOMINION

An Apocalyptic Epic in Seven Books

I0665457

BOOK V

ASCENSION

by

Compasse

Sacrata Dei Press

A Division of The Compasse Corporation

Front Cover Art: *Fettering Star*, by Ben Hamrick

Back Cover Art: *Paradise Lost 14*, by Gustave Doré

Printed in the United States of America

For John Karol Mary, Jacinta Christopher, Gianna Anthony,
& David Guadalupe;

I pray that I may one day see the marvelous vision that you now
embrace...

Author's Note

Are we truly free?

When we speak of freedom, we are generally referring to the ability to make choices for ourselves unfettered by coercive or limiting external forces. Most thinking people understand that freedom is not merely "doing what I want, when I want"—that is more accurately defined as *license*, and it carries the simple problem that one person's license will necessarily infringe on another's freedom. For that reason, the "freedom" of any member of a society is always necessarily tempered (with great and thoughtful care) by the general needs of the common good for all.

But when we speak here of being free, we are considering more (though not exclusively) the issue of *interior* freedom. The reality of love and even the "problem of evil" are deeply intertwined within this concept of freedom, or more specifically put, free will. Truly, neither is possible without it, and our capacity to act within our free will has serious ramifications for each of us, which I would like to examine in brief here.

Our intellect works in concert with our will. If we believe that we have the ability to reason, then we understand that through reason, thinking people can choose one option over another; it can be as mundane as chocolate over vanilla, or as important as whether or not to terminate the life of one's unborn child. Within a person possessing a well-formed conscience, the intellect at times will serve as a mitigating force for the will. Working together, especially when sound reason suggests a course of action which goes against the desires of our interior drives, the intellect and will function in a manner which is authentically free, as opposed to permitting us to become a slave to their appetites.

The reason this question of our interior freedom is so important in this day and age may not be readily apparent, but it manifests itself in the more common question: "Am I responsible for my actions?" Choices are always before us, and most would agree that we are responsible to the degree that we are free to make those choices. If the case can be made that we do *not* have the capacity to exercise our free will, then justice demands that we *not* be held accountable. If we are not free, natural consequences, instead of being an existential corrective force, are nothing more than a grossly unfair twist of fate.

Yet the majority of us would attest to the fact that, at the very least, we have the *possibility* or even *potential* to be free. We understand that acting "freely" does not mean we act without any influences on our emotions or intellect; yes, being raised by abusive alcoholic parents will very possibly leave us with a malformed conscience and limited impulse control. But despite these factors that may fetter our interior freedom to some degree, most would still agree that they are not adequate defenses or justifications when the subject, say, commits rape, murder, or another inherently heinous act that brings harm to another. There is something within us that still attests that this person had *some* capacity (a.k.a. "freedom") to *not* commit the act.

Now, the issue of whether or not we are free, and therefore whether or not we should be subject to consequences, is most significant when we are dealing with the concept of Divine Judgment. Can it be just for a person to receive eternal punishment for a temporal act? For that matter, are we sufficiently "free" in the finite world to make an informed choice with potentially infinite consequences? And finally, if this great deity has the ability to see all time at once, knowing what our choices would be before He even created us, does His knowledge of our future actions actually impede our freedom to carry them out? Could it not mean, in some sense, that we are all then predestined for heaven or hell?

This leads us to the critical question, one that essentially drives to the crux of the matter: "Can we trust that an all-loving God would provide a sufficient measure of freedom to even those who, by the claims of ancient prophecy, seem 'destined' to certain acts *against* love in living out their part in the human drama?"

– *Compasse*

...*from* Requiem

A year has passed, and we meet Sister Sawlus, assistant editor of Mystic Realism's newspaper, "The Signs of the Times", her son, Caleb, and her mate, Siro Scribner, chief editor and now full supporter of the cause. The curtain rises as Çön Razón, the evangelical band of Jimi T. Expo, counting Nathaniel Freeman-Page among its members, ignites the world with its music and message, drawing in the masses. It is clear that Nathaniel has made some concessions in order to achieve his dream of the "big time", as The Seal of Mystic Realism now indelibly marks his hand.

Father Daniel Ananias is now accompanied by the young Phineas Savoie, a Cajun/Creole former gang member who, after experiencing a profound conversion, now possesses a supernatural gift of insight and knowledge. The gift curiously links Phineas to the fatherless Caleb, whose craving for masculine attention deepens the bond, though Caleb becomes increasingly torn as the words from this "dark man" are incongruent with those of his mother. Father Daniel and Phineas place themselves at the service of "Providence", attempting to mitigate the influence of the counter-Christian forces.

We watch as Mystic Realism starts to seep into not only music, but business, politics, and especially the media. More and more newspapers, corporations, and politicians officially proclaim their allegiance to the cause as thousands flee from the "archaic" monotheistic religions for a worldview which affirms their worldly desires and seemingly follows the precepts of good human reason. Miraculous cures are being witnessed through the Mystic King, while subtle—and sometimes not so subtle—persecutions of other religions, especially Christianity, begin to take place. Men of power who stand in opposition to "The Way" learn that they are doing so at their own peril.

Nathaniel, while trying to stay faithful to the cause, continues to find himself tormented by visions of Jesse. His disillusionment with the fame and fortune he so craved leads him deeper and deeper into despair, moving slowly towards a vegetative depression. He continues to utilize all his resources to track down his old friend Simon, likenesses of whom lurk in the shadows, eluding the increasingly unstable rock star. Following a particularly severe anxiety attack (which continue to increase in frequency) Nathaniel receives assistance from a paramedic, Ralph Tobit, but is reticent to seek continued support from this man, as it is clear that he is a Christian. Nathaniel quietly struggles with unanswered questions as he reflects upon the paramedic's seemingly altruistic motives.

Sister Sawlus, on the other hand, finds her connection with Mystic Realism growing stronger as she joyfully watches her son, Caleb, grow in the 'faith'. She feels twice blessed, as the Mystic King himself takes a personal interest in the boy. Though also plagued by images of her past, Sawlus is able to refocus herself quickly through her hatred of the Christians and their staunch opposition to the cause.

The ever-meddling Tæsír Hoc (Luther) finds himself more and more in tension with the ways of Jimi T., believing the so-called 'Anointed's' initiatives to bring order to the world are counterproductive to his own efforts to sow chaos. Luther's concern spreads among the Illumini, who now allow for the possibility that the Mystic King is functioning under his own agenda… and perhaps has even experienced a change of heart.

President Hugh Jennings Lang struggles to emerge from a deep sense of despair, not yet being able to come to terms with the loss of his entire family. A potential solution presents itself in the soothing music of Çön Razón, which seems to provide temporary consolation to the beleaguered president, though the diversion quickly digresses into an obsessive crutch. Yet after being confronted by British Prime Minister Sir Thomas Leese, Lang is able to "break the spell," though his liberation is short-lived, as Luther orchestrates the demise of the once popular president, and Senator William Maison is sworn in as his successor.

Andrey Gavrilenkov continues to be tormented by his dreams of the Beslan Massacre, where he lost his wife and two of his daughters. In desperation, he approaches Mikey Logiarato for assistance in locating his last surviving daughter, Sascha Luneska, who is clearly "in deep" with The Way of Mystic Realism and makes it clear that she has no interest in abandoning this 'liberated' life.

Mikhail Ostankino further to builds his empire of organized crime in South and Central America, though learns that he has been diagnosed with an aggressive form of lung cancer.

Annie D. Nesterov is besieged by guilt and self-loathing, recognizing the horrible consequences of her act of unforgiveness towards her now-deceased husband, Alexandre. When Father Daniel is transferred to a small town in upstate New York, Annie D. ponders his offer to serve with him there. She sells all she has, and is about to depart from the autobus station when she seemingly encounters a specter from her past; Vlad Ivankov, her husband's supposedly dead boss of old, steps onto an executive autobus from an adjacent platform and departs, ignoring Annie D.'s calls. She is left standing on the platform, more ambivalent than ever as to what God is asking of her.

The book closes with three climatic scenes; a confrontation between the enigmatic paramedic named Ralph and the Mystic King, an inebriated and hate-filled Simon emerging to encounter a face from the past—real or imagined—we are left to ponder, and a distraught and suicidal Nathaniel Freeman-Page seeking release as he steps from the roof of a building overlooking the busy streets of Los Angeles…

ASCENSION

It was not long that Rahmat opened his eyes again. From the side of the horizon and in the direction of Quibla, a group of travelers were coming toward him. As they were getting closer, Rahmat could hear people singing. He listened carefully, "va lA tahsaban-nal-lazina ghoteloo..." the song said.

As the group got closer to him he noticed that most of them were walking on foot, some camels were carrying women and children and some soldiers were riding the horses. As they reached near Rahmat, a strong man in front of the group raised his hand to stop the travelers. The columns of hundreds of people stopped and silence took over. Rahmat saw somebody coming towards him. Again the smell of flowers filled the air.

"Salam Rahmat, my son. This group [ghAfeleh] will be traveling very far, and on its way is going to visit Karbala. I understand that you are coming with us."

Rahmat was shocked. How were these people going to Karbala? The whole area was full of mines and Iraqi soldiers. Besides, Karbala was under control of the Ba'athi regime. He tried to say something but he was very weak [from his wounds]. Suddenly, he heard the voice of a small girl as she was coming toward the man.

"Father, is this young man coming with us?"

"Yes my darling Sakineh, he is one of us."

– Abu Mohammed Salar-A-azam
Waiting for the Reappearance

1

Here we go round the prickly pear
Prickly pear prickly pear
Here we go round the prickly pear
At five o'clock in the morning.

– t.s. eliot
The Hollow Men

i

"But how can this happen?" Sir Thomas Louis Leese, Chairman of the United League of Democratic Nations and soon-to-be *former* Prime Minister of Great Britain, inquired.

"It's in the law, Tom," his colleague responded. "You do not have to run, or even be on the ballot, to be elected. Kind of curious, I would say... and definitely not without plenty of juicy tidbits for public fodder!"

Sir Thomas locked his wheelchair into his assigned parliamentary spot, giving only peripheral attention to the comments of his colleague. There were still a few minutes before the scheduled opening of the new session of the House of Commons.

"How do you mean?"

His colleague, one who found conspiracy in just about everything, leaned in toward him, speaking barely above a whisper. "Well, his ascension to this position relied heavily on a series of seemingly minor and obscure amendments to parliamentary law—amendments passed more than twenty years ago. These statutes impacted eligibility and it seems alternate means of election as well. A bit suspicious, wouldn't you say?"

Sir Thomas frowned. "But I was unaware that he was even a British citizen." He began to sift through his papers, attempting to appear less intrigued—or even concerned—than he was.

"Apparently so..." his colleague continued. "According to records, he's maintained dual citizenship, here and in the United States, since his adoption shortly after his birth in Romania. His English heritage is unmistakable in his speech." He looked out momentarily to the entry doors to the chambers, chuckling. "Still, Tom, no need to fret... it's *only* the House of Commons... not what it used to be, at least since your high and mighty U.L.D.N." At this point the colleague paused momentarily to see if Sir Thomas was sharing the same intrigue. The prime minister's distracted expression suggested he was not. "But really, Tom, your days here are numbered... the next coalition government should be in place in no more than a few months. Why should you really concern yourself?"

Sir Thomas completed his feigned interest in the straightening of his papers and looked at his colleague with a slight grin. "Well, the way my nephew Adam speaks of him, you'd think he was the Second Coming." Then, in an attempt to make light of the situation—if for no one else other than himself—he intoned, "Still, the day a rock star gets elected to the House of Commons is the day I start playing the drums."

His colleague smiled as some commotion at the entrance of the chambers caught both of their attention. "Well, Tom, you better get your bloody sticks out because there he is."

Sir Thomas looked up to lay his eyes on the so-called Mystic King in the flesh for the first time. Jimi T. Expo stood at the entrance in a perfectly cut suit, his hair and face impeccably groomed, and sporting a pair of old-style dark sunglasses. The room fell silent, then several members stood and began to applaud. A few more followed, then a few more. In less than thirty seconds, nearly the entire House was giving their newest, and perhaps most unlikely, member a standing ovation.

Sir Thomas looked to his colleague with an expression of amused curiosity, only to receive the beginnings of an apprehensive look in return. Though standing would have been appropriate, his wounds from battles past kept him restrained to his wheelchair. Still, even from his seated position, Sir Thomas was immediately spotted by Jimi T., who then embarked on his trek down the aisle. The applause began to subside; yet all members remained standing.

The prime minister felt his heart rate slowly accelerate as this man approached. Sir Thomas Leese, the man who had stood up to any and all forces of adversity without so much of a flinch, felt uneasy… even… *nervous.*

Jimi T. reached his place in front of Sir Thomas and stopped. There was a brief anticipatory pause before the so-called Mystic King spoke.

"Good day, Prime Minister. I am Jimi T. Expo, and I humbly place myself at your service."

Sir Thomas bowed his head slightly in acknowledgement with a somewhat manufactured expression of serenity. The fact was, at this point, his insides were clearly anything but serene.

"Welcome, my good man. This is quite a pleasure, I must say. And if you do not mind my asking, would you do me the honor of removing your sunglasses so that I may look upon the eyes of my newest colleague in service?"

The globally familiar trace of a smile emerged on Jimi T.'s face. "Forgive me, Sir Thomas, but I am afraid that a childhood accident has left me without the ability to expose my eyes to the light. But I would like to convey to you my deepest admiration, and I feel honored that you would call me 'colleague'."

Sir Thomas nodded, maintaining the same pleasant but neutral expression on his face. The Mystic King extended his hand, and he followed suit.

"It is good to finally meet you, and please forgive me for not standing… as God would permit, I am confined for the duration."

"Perhaps a chance of fate does not have the final word."

Their hands clasped and then…

A bolt like electricity shot through Sir Thomas' whole body before descending to resonate in his legs. A sensation of warmth emanated through his thighs… then his calves… then his feet and toes. His eyes locked with whatever lay behind those dark sunglasses.

I could stand…

Sir Thomas struggled to maintain a steady expression.

"Will you not receive the gift?"

He sensed the hair on the back of his neck stand up, as his entire body now felt enveloped by the strange warmth. Yet at this juncture in his life, he was too wise, too resolute in his understanding that *nothing* came without a price—especially that which is described as a 'gift'.

"I will not stand!"

And the moment broke. The sensation quickly dissipated, and Jimi T. cocked his head in a visible expression of curiosity. Sir Thomas quickly ensured that no noticeable time would pass.

"If you please, Mr. Expo, join us at your place here, which has been prepared for you."

A loud clap of thunder crashed in the distance as an unsuspecting world moved on.

ii

Phineas Savoie knocked on the door to Father Daniel Ananias' rectory office before poking his head in.

"Father?"

The priest looked up from his Bible. There was another man seated near him, and Phineas recognized him as the holy man that had visited them at the seminary on the day when a handful of young men had been discerned for a special role in what was to come. Despite the holy man's clearly devout nature, Phineas still was a bit distracted by the overgrown beard and religious habit made of sackcloth.

"Oh... *Mo chagren*, Father... I didn't realize that you had—"

Father Daniel waved him off. "It is okay, Phinny. I am sure you remember Brother Hanoch... he has been with the Christian Resistance since before it even had such a name. What is it you wanted?"

Phineas stepped into the room. "*Mais*, ahh... it's Terry Aborn. He's here and says you summoned him."

"Oh yes," Father Daniel responded. His tone had quickly become uncharacteristically grim. "Please send him in."

Phineas left, and Father Daniel's expression grew stern. He glanced briefly at Hanoch, who sat to his left. "Terry's a leader of the resistance in Stowe, Ohio. I sent for him two days ago."

At that moment, Terrence Aborn burst into the room with a disconcerted Phineas several steps behind him. Aborn bore a large grin on his face—almost too large. "Danny-boy! Good to see you!"

He walked up to Father Daniel, who had barely enough time to stand before Aborn gave him a bear hug, almost lifting him off his feet. Father Daniel gave him a halfhearted hug back, which did not go unnoticed by Aborn. He released the priest, stepped away, and looked curiously at Father Daniel's emotionless expression.

"What's going on, Danny?"

"Sit down, Terry."

Aborn hesitated, glancing suspiciously at Father Daniel's guest as he obliged the priest's request. He chuckled uncomfortably. "Come on, Danny, what's this all about?"

Father Daniel sat down across from him, placing his clasped hands on the table. He took a moment to gather his thoughts, then leaned forward.

"It has come to my attention that not only were you responsible for the death of a trainer in the *Neo Mîstè*, but you have encouraged others in your following to do the same. I even heard a rumor that you have put a price on the head of the journalist known as Sister Sawlus."

Father Daniel leaned further towards Aborn, who seemed unfazed. "What in God's name do you think you are doing?"

The transformation in Aborn's disposition was immediate. He stood, placing his hands on the desk opposite Father Daniel's, a sense of intensity growing in his face. "Exactly, Danny... in the name of God! Damn bastards are out there corrupting our youth. They're *killing* our defenseless children, Danny. Not like just killing their bodies, but worse—killing their very *souls*! What I did was nothing short of slaying a demon... and if this act saves even one child's soul, then it is worth it!"

Father Daniel stood himself. The meek and humble priest was clearly unintimidated and attempted to restrain his anger. "Have you lost your mind, Terry? Has the Church taught you nothing? We do not combat evil with evil!"

Aborn lifted his arms in disbelief. "I can't believe what I'm hearing! We are at war! Do you expect me to just lie down and watch them destroy innocent life? I will not, Danny. I will not stand still and let this happen!"

Father Daniel then did something that Phineas had never seen him do before. He gritted his teeth and leaned forward until his face was no more than a decimeter from Aborn's. "I realize that you will do what you will. But you will *not* do it as part of the Church. The Body will not condone your behavior, and neither do I."

Aborn looked at the priest in utter incredulity. "Are you saying what I think you're saying, Danny? Are you trying to tell me I'm being excommunicated? Because I don't recognize your authority to—"

"It is by *God's* authority that I am speaking to you right now. It is *you* that bring this upon yourself by *your* actions. You must cease and desist from this behavior immediately and beseech God for forgiveness for the horrible misdeeds you have committed! If you do not, then you are no longer of the Body."

Aborn fell silent and returned to his chair, pondering intensely as he shook his head. Phineas looked uncomfortably at Father Daniel but did not have his eyes met. The man called Hanoch looked at Aborn, the sadness in his eyes quite evident.

After a brief period of severe silence, Aborn shook his head one final time and stood up. "You're going to lose this war—like the fools that you are. The Bible says that the righteous must drive out the evildoers. Yet you are here wasting time battling one of your own." Aborn looked at the other two men in the room with an unnerving expression, then back at Father Daniel. "I realize now, Danny, that I sit here amongst cowards. Cowards who are afraid to put their faith into action and go *all* the way in combating this scourge upon the Earth. You are neither hot nor cold—you are the lukewarm which the Lord spews out!"

Aborn took a brief moment to once again attempt to stare down each of the men in the room. "I pity you! I pity you all—for you are already defeated!"

With that, he moved towards the exit, brushing past Phineas and slamming the door on his way out. Phineas looked at Father Daniel, clearly dismayed. His priest and mentor sighed as he slumped back down in his chair, rubbing his eyes with his thumb and forefinger. Phineas stepped towards Father Daniel and Hanoch, seating himself in the chair previously occupied by Aborn.

"Father, forgive me, but I don't understand. If indeed the death of one man prevents him from leading any more children into the hands of the Evil One, then couldn't it be an acceptable... even a *good* thing?"

Father Daniel looked up at his naïve apprentice and shook his head gently. "That is not God's way, Phinny. If we are to call ourselves Christian, then we must *always* strive to be Christian, no matter what the circumstances. We cannot sell our souls even for what can appear to be great victories in battle.

ASCENSION

When we give up what makes us disciples of Christ in order to achieve what may seem a desirable end, we are doing Satan's bidding. Every step towards our goal must be taken in *God's* way. There are no shortcuts to salvation."

Phineas looked intently at his mentor and nodded. "*Mo konmprann,* Father." With that he stood and exited the room.

A moment later, Hanoch turned to the still pensive Father Daniel Ananias. "He is quite a gifted young man. It is clear that God has a strong calling upon him."

Father Daniel nodded absently.

"You shared with me sometime back that he offered a special access to the woman. What has come of that?"

Father Daniel did not immediately reply, his mind still elsewhere.

"Father?"

The priest turned with a start. "Eh...? Oh, I am sorry, Brother Hanoch. We continue to pray for her. Yes, Phinny has provided a... a *unique* access to this woman, which perhaps has prevented some major setbacks against God's purpose. Yet the truth be known... and I am little ashamed to admit, that in our zealousness I fear we have overstepped our bounds. I must take to heart my own words."

With that, Hanoch looked back towards the door, reflecting on the angry and misled soul which had stormed out. "The lure of the enemy's ways is strong. History is riddled with justifications of many acts under the banner of 'a lesser evil'." He then looked back to Father Daniel. "What you have done here is both just and necessary. We are by no means pacifists—evil must be stood against. Often we must take the more difficult path... and leave the rest to God."

iii

The massive throng filled Saint Peter's Square as Pope Peter II approached on foot. The boat, supplied ceremoniously by former members of the Sicilian Mafia, had taken the Pontiff and a small contingent from his exile on the Isle of Patmos to the port of Rome, then up the Tiber River before disembarking. The seventy-year-old Peter had insisted on walking the final kilometer.

DOMINION

Many of the supporters, until recently a very silent near majority, held up images of Our Lady of Fátima, celebrating the anniversary of the final appearance of the mother of Jesus to three young children in the small Portuguese town. Their cheers were deafening, and Peter, with Msgr. Craig Ebright at his side, smiled broadly, attempting not to provide any display of the considerable pain he was in. Several more of the mysterious boils, not unlike those that had riddled the body of his friend, Andreas II, had emerged in the past month. But this would not be his focus today.

Peter blessed the crowd as he walked among them. Though mid-October, thousands waved palm branches imported for the occasion. He leaned over to his assistant and friend.

"It is good to be back home, is it not, Monsignor?"

But Msgr. Craig was a bit more cautious as his eyes darted across the crowd, betraying his feigned enthusiastic expression. "I don't know, Holy Father. The truth is I don't feel safe, and I don't trust the Caliph's motives for permitting your return."

They continued to walk down a human corridor lined with a thousand newly commissioned members of the Swiss Guard. Peter offered a slight bow of his head in acknowledgement as they approached the final turn before stepping onto Vatican soil. "I do not need to tell you, Monsignor, that our trust is in no man—only in God."

Msgr. Craig nodded. "His will be done, Your Holiness."

The two, along with their contingent, turned the corner so they now were at the threshold of Saint Peter's Square. The crowd erupted even louder, at which point they saw three men standing on a dais at the top of the steps leading to the Basilica. Peter and Msgr. Craig immediately recognized the first two as Ibn Fatimah and the Imam himself... though it was a few moments before the identity of the third man became evident.

"Well," the Pontiff breathed with a slightly strained smile, "this is quite unexpected."

Standing on the top of the dais, Caliph Ali Bakr whispered to Tæsír Hoc without diverting his gaze, while a distracted Ibn Fatimah waved to the crowd.

"I truly hope the Anointed knows what he is doing in permitting this. Things here are already tenuous at best, and this could be the final boost the

Cortät need to organize their insurgence."

The Prophet nodded slightly in acknowledgement, he too avoiding the impression of a conversation. "I am not clear as to his purpose, but at the very least, the rat has been drawn out of his hole of protection."

Tæsír Hoc tried to avoid a clear expression of disdain as the broadly smiling Pontiff waved to his many followers while they threw their palms at his feet.

"What an ass…"

iv

A great rupture manifested itself, as war broke out among the subjects of the Sovereign's Kingdom.

A third of the Kingdom aligned in rebellion under their Counter-Sovereign, Lumenel. At his right hand fought Chumael, along with three other members of the Sovereign's former Choir.

The counter-melody was deafening… soul piercing, disintegrating, yet still peculiarly alluring. The *absence* had not only grown but become an entity unto itself.

Machiel, despite his rank being far below that of Lumenel, held the favor of the Sovereign and led those forces still loyal to His way against the mystical insurgence. The line had been drawn, and each subject freely chose his place of standing. There would be none left neutral in this battle.

And it came to pass that the conflict spilled beyond the Kingdom as the forces of Lumenel made war against the most vulnerable of the Sovereign's children. Standing on the threshold of perpetuity, Lumenel called out to his disciple Chumael.

"It is you, Chumael, whom I chose to lead our forces beyond the Kingdom."

Chumael bowed. "By your command, my lord."

"The inhabitants of this land are wretched, yet they are the prized possession of the Sovereign. I have been to their land and have found them to be feeble, as I foretold. They *will* follow us… and the Sovereign will then see clearly that His Plan—though admittedly noble—was naïve and ill-begotten.

His Kingdom will fall, and a new kingdom... one of liberation and strength... will arise!"

The two envisioned the new order with relish. Their place in history was assured. Lumenel spoke again.

"The Sovereign has peculiarly hidden His face in all of this... perhaps His shame prevents His intervention in this matter. Nonetheless, I must depart to engage the forces of Machiel, and I will crush him. You must go, Chumael, to this carnal land. Gather whoever you can—take whatever is not freely given, and find the woman. The Sovereign's plan foolishly hinges upon her. She is with child... and it will be this child that I will devour... only then will our victory be consummated."

"And what of Rephiel?"

"He is there... I bound him for a season, from which he has since emerged. But he is vulnerable... impotent. If you find him there, you must give no quarter. Then he must be given the choice..."

2

i

"You promised me that you'd accompany me to the Pulitzer award ceremony."

It was clear that Sawlus was incensed, though she was not unaware of the fact that she was touching on a very sensitive topic.

"Don't you think friendship... after such a senseless tragedy... trumps an award ceremony?" Siro demanded, not ready to give in on this one—at least not yet.

"I think you're overstating your relationship, dear. Getting high with someone does not a bond make. Besides, you already attended the funer—the *Çlausür* I mean. "

Now it was Siro's turn to be angry. "We did a lot more than 'just get high' together, Sawlus! And he deserved better than any of this. I'm just doing my part. All of his associates will be there... and I know he would want me there for the... for the..."

"The *Récræ Tüm.*"

Both Siro and Sawlus were startled by Caleb's interjection, not realizing he had entered the room. He stood at the threshold of the kitchen dressed in his red uniform of the *Ñeø Mįştè*, his head still hairless, with an expression of mild astonishment on his face.

"It is the celebration of one of the Saved's re-entry into time and space, one hundred and fifty days following their transitory absorption into the *Kôles*. It is a reminder that death is not the end but only a new beginning—a new cycle—on this plane of existence. This is clearly taught by Tæsír Leviat in *Lib Dône Verü*."

Caleb looked sternly at his mother—as sternly as a six-year-old could anyway. "Uncle Sy is right, Mother. He must go as both support and affirmation of this reality. I am quite surprised that you would suggest differently, for the affirmation of men."

Sawlus looked down, clearly embarrassed to be admonished by anyone, let alone by her son. Yet she knew his words to be true. The boy was gifted, and his connection with the *Kôles* seemed to grow by the hour. She nodded and then looked to Siro.

"You're right... you're both right. I will be on that plane for Los Angeles with you tonight. In fact, in honor of your friend, we will *all* celebrate the *Récræ Tüm*."

ii

Sir Thomas Leese took the last bite of his self-made masterpiece-of-an-omelet as he looked across the table at his nephew. Adam consumed his pancakes with a vengeance as he immersed himself in his newly acquired graphic novel, *The Life of Thomas More*. The boy was quite the Renaissance man, shunning the much more interactive and entertaining eBooks that his classmates so enjoyed. Behind Adam, Sir Thomas was able to gaze out at the still breathtaking scenery of the Dundalk Bay, visible from nearly all corners of his Blackrock, Ireland vacation cottage.

It had been their solemn annual tradition, attending Mass together on All Souls' Day, praying for the salvation of Adam's deceased parents, and then following it up with a massive, home-cooked brunch. It seemed to also be part of this annual tradition that Sir Thomas would find himself drawn into a deep reverie; an opportunity for clarity—for perspective—where he could step back and reflect on the many complex dimensions of the world and how his one life fit into it all.

Am I making a difference?

ASCENSION

He reflected on the events of the past year: another personal loss, with the assassination of his friend and confidant, Hugh Jennings Lang; the return of the Holy Father to Rome; the ascension of this 'Pied Piper' of the masses, Jimi T. Expo, to a position of political legitimacy; and now this impending crisis with the crumbling Eurabia—perhaps even the entire Islamic Union. All of these situations demanded a response, and as the Chairman of the United League of Democratic Nations, it was clear Sir Thomas would not be able to do what so many others seemed to be doing—and take a pass on these matters.

Or could I? For once, could someone else carry this burden?

He knew, in reality, that he was by no means alone in this battle. Even with the loss of Hugh, and subsequently the United States, his friends and allies in the U.L.D.N. continued to be a source of encouragement. But would their resolve be so strong in the impending confrontation within the once free Europe, especially without the support of the United States?

"Uncle?"

Sir Thomas almost jumped at the word coming from Adam's lips. He quickly turned his gaze to the boy, who was now well into adolescence (as he constantly needed to remind his overprotective uncle) in his fourteenth year.

"Yes, Adam?"

"You zoned out again, Uncle. Am I to expect this to be a normal occurrence, young man? It seems not becoming of the leader of the free world, I would think."

The interior tension dissipated from Sir Thomas' spirit as a soft chuckle escaped his lips. "No, it is not becoming at all, is it? I'm sorry, Adam, there is much on my mind."

"And I suppose much less on mine, Uncle. But you used to smile a lot more—even when things were difficult. Is there something bad coming our way?"

Sir Thomas thought long and hard before responding. He had never gone to great lengths to shelter the boy from the realities of the world. After having your parents taken from you in your first week out of the womb, what more was there to be sheltered from?

"Well, Adam… actually, yes, it does seem that some tough times are ahead—potentially dark times. It seems there are very troubling matters which I need to attend to, even in my last days leading both Great Britain and the U.L.D.N."

The boy looked at his uncle steadily. Despite his fleeting interest in both sport figures and even the Mystic King himself, there was no question who his true hero was.

"I suppose it boils down to… I am hesitant to begin something that I may not be able to finish. The objective may be clear, though the outcome is uncertain at best. But the one thing I *am* certain of is that the cost will be great."

Adam continued to look at his uncle, clearly taking in the severity of his words, yet at the same time remaining unshaken. He placed his fork down, and folding his hands, leaned forward and spoke with a tone of conviction not common in one his age.

"You have always taught me to stand firm in what is right, Uncle. No matter what the sacrifice…" he paused only momentarily as he glanced up to the picture on the wall—the single image of both his parents holding him at his birth, "…and no matter what the cost…"

iii

Ibn Fatimah paced nervously back and forth. Eliot Kohein Lige sat in the chair before Ibn's desk, observing his Muslim friend as he wrestled with a major dilemma.

"I do not know how much longer I can hold out, my friend. The Caliph—he continues to be a complete enigma to me! Having that religious impostor present with us at the Pontiff's return—it is unthinkable!" Ibn stopped momentarily, holding a clear expression of distaste on his face. He looked back to Eli. "The Islamic Union is crumbling, and Eurabia is certain to be the first to go. The Caliph requires a scapegoat for all of this. At this point, I have no doubt that I will serve in that role for him."

Eli nodded in sad acknowledgement. "I see what is happening, Ibn, and I hope it is also evident to you that this is *his* doing. We must stand strong in what is right." He paused a moment longer before speaking again. "Do you believe that the Caliph identifying you as the one responsible for all that is failing in the Islamic Union will be sufficient to prevent its collapse?"

Ibn did not hesitate, shaking his head. "No… I do not. Its fall is inevitable, and I am sure he is not blind to that. But it *will* buy the Caliph some time to consolidate his power. I am not sure how he plans to do it, yet I am certain there will be a cascading effect among other Islamic provinces. Perhaps he will fall back to Mecca... I do not know. What I am assured of, however, is that he is not without a plan."

The two sat in silence as multiple scenarios of destruction began to materialize within their minds. It was Eli who finally broke the stillness.

"Is there no way out for you, my friend?"

Ibn looked back at Eli with troubled eyes. "I fear there is not. I believe the die has been cast, as they say. In the greater scheme, my life is insignificant... though I must act in accord with my conscience at this juncture, regardless of how my life and intentions are portrayed—regardless of what is to come."

Once again a silent, even prayerful moment emerged between the two, though it seemed that something even more transcendent was taking place within this affiliation. Without prompting, however, the sense of despair slowly seemed to lift from the room, as if the reigning darkness had been pierced, even if only for a moment.

Ibn sighed deeply. He looked to the floor like a man carrying the weight of ages upon him, but there now seemed to be a hint of... *hope* his voice. "You know, Christian, we profess to serve the one God, the same God of Abraham."

Eli nodded. "Yes we do."

"Yet you give the man Jesus much greater importance than we."

Eli again nodded. "Yes, we do. He is the Christ, the Son of the Living God."

Ibn smiled sadly. "You speak as if you have met him."

It was Eli's turn to look downward, remaining silent.

Ibn continued, but this time in a more careful fashion. "I belong to the ways of the Prophet Mohammed—may peace be upon him—my friend. I have been a Muslim all my life. Yet... I must confess... of recent times, I have had dreams..."

"Dreams?"

"Yes, dreams that seem to be more than dreams. I see a woman in blue... yet she is clothed in the sun. The world is below her feet and twelve stars surround her head. She is with child, and she beckons to me."

Eli held Ibn's stare steadily.

"…and I must further confess… I know… I know it was you…"

At once Eli's expression transformed into one of utter confusion. "What do you mean?"

"Atop Mount Moriah… when the quake hit. I was just a boy, and I could not even see your face, but I *know* it was you… of this I am certain."

Again Eli did not speak, he only looked into the eyes of his friend with understanding—even compassion—for what was to come.

"I do not pretend to know the will of Allah, nor His ways. I do not understand why all these things happen, Christian. Yet now as I am short for this world, I cannot help but think…"

Eli looked up, one eyebrow raised, as Ibn struggled to find the words that spoke what his heart was feeling.

"…I cannot help but think that had I not been raised Muslim, I would have greatly enjoyed worshipping the One True God together with you in your Assembly…"

3

CAIRO, Egypt - Ibn Fatimah, one-time Foreign Minister of the Islamic Union, was killed yesterday at the hands of an incensed Islamic mob following an internationally broadcast press conference by the Caliph Ali Bakr.

The public disclosure by the so-called 12th Imam claimed irrefutable evidence revealed that, at the dawn of the Islamic Revolution, it was actually Fatimah who tipped the British to the invasion of their homeland by Islamic soldiers. Bakr provided "irrefutable evidence" that, at the outset, detailed plans were provided by Fatimah to an undisclosed associate of Prime Minister Sir Thomas Leese. Based on this information, Leese was able to stop the incursion by destroying the Channel Tunnel, sending over a million Muslim fighters to their deaths.

At the time of the Caliph's announcement, it was related that security forces were attempting to take the former foreign minister into custody but were delayed due to continued civil unrest. This delay provided Islamic vigilantes with the opportunity to carry out the death sentence on Fatimah. Of curious note, unconfirmed reports state that Fatimah was found with a brown scapular around his neck, a charm commonly worn by Christian religionists.

Despite the Caliph's apparent attempts to utilize the so-called 'greatest act of treason in the history of Islam' to re-ignite unity among the imploding provinces of the Islamic Union, the revelation has actually served as an incendiary force within Eurabia, which is now in a state of near-complete anarchy. Widespread rioting and violence has been reported in all major cities.

DOMINION

i

Phineas walked cautiously through the maze of mirrors. Thousands of reflections of his own image stared back at him, some not quite in full synchronization with his movements. Though somewhat unnerving, over the years he had grown accustomed to the unsettling nature of his visions.

He had been obedient to his mentor in not initiating contact with the boy once it had become clear that this act was not in conformance with God's will. Yet he would still see the boy at times as Phineas sat on the outskirts of his uninitiated visions. For the most part, he only observed the boy frolicking in the playground of his own dreamscape. Yet at other times, their eyes would lock, though no discernable communication would pass between them.

Today, however, Phineas immediately sensed something different. Though he had never closed himself off to their shared vision—as Providence presented—he had a clear sense that he himself had been... *summoned* on this occasion. Could the boy have learned to call upon the images on his own so quickly?

ASCENSION

Phineas' anxiety began to build, but gratefully dissipated as he stepped into the clearing. There in the center of the mystical playground stood the boy.

"Bonjou, Caleb," Phineas called out, a sense of relief evident in his tone.

Yet the boy did not verbally respond, only raising a single hand, as if in solemn greeting. Phineas began to move more briskly towards him, then slowed when he saw the expression on Caleb's face.

"What's wrong, Caleb?" he inquired, his anxiety slowly returning.

He continued to look at Caleb, who maintained an expression indicative of shame or guilt. Caleb looked down.

"Why do you wish to bring harm to my mother?"

Phineas was momentarily taken off-guard by the smoothness of the boy's speech. But even more so, he found himself perplexed by the question posed.

"Oh, sha-sha, pod nah. Who told you I want to hurt your mother, Caleb? I want to…"

But his voice trailed off as an ominous figure emerged from behind the boy. Phineas' stomach dropped as he came face to face with the man who had come to be known as the Mystic King.

"It is I who have enlightened the boy." He spoke in a voice which reverberated throughout the scene. *"Identify yourself before me… I see that you bear the mark of the Dìshalâk."*

Phineas, though wanting desperately to appear strong in the presence of this perceived great evil, stammered. *"I-I d-don't have to answer that."*

A disconcerting trace of a smile emerged on the figure's face. *"I am afraid you may have to answer for much more than that, young man. I will not tolerate your filling my son's mind with lies…"*

Phineas' eyes narrowed, sensing the fallacy of this last statement *"That's not true… he is not your son. He is the son of—"*

"SILENCE!" the figure boomed.

For just an instant, Phineas thought he saw the slightest twinge of anger slip across the figure's face. A moment later, however, it was gone, leaving Phineas to ponder if he had only imagined it.

"My very confused young man, it is very…saddening to hear you attempt to speak of truth. But take solace, you will be given a choice, and in that, I will cut your days short so that

you will not suffer the turmoil of what is to come."

Phineas' mouth fell open, but he was unable to summon a response to what he had just heard. He then saw movement to the left of the Mystic King, perhaps a dozen meters behind him. It was a figure—a figure of a woman, whose silhouette carried a sense of... *familiarity* about it. Phineas suddenly realized that he was sweating profusely, as his gaze darted back to the Mystic King. He reached up to wipe his forehead, but when his hand returned, he saw that it was smeared with some type of ink.

"I seek only your liberation, young man... I seek to free you from the shackles of a dying myth..."

Phineas, at this point fully at a loss as to what the Mystic King was saying, turned to look at his reflection in the thousands of mirrors which continued to surround the scene. His heart fell in horror as he saw that the mark of the Christian Elect was smeared and dripping right off his forehead. He turned back, stunned, at the pair who seemed to now enjoy full dominion over this vision.

"Your fight is admirable, young man, but it is sadly misguided."

Caleb looked back at Phineas. The boy turned briefly towards the mysterious feminine figure in the shadows, then back to Phineas. A smile emerged from his face, slowly growing into a grin, and soon a chuckle emerged from Caleb's once-innocent face. A moment followed, then the boy fell into an uncontrollable fit of laughter.

ii

The battle for Europe was surprisingly brief, taking only three weeks for full occupation by U.L.D.N. forces and the general end of active military operations, save a few isolated skirmishes within the now former-Islamic province. In truth, it seemed that the majority of the residents were relieved to the see the three million "peacekeepers" emerge on the scene. The United States—now being part of the North American Union which included Canada and Mexico—had predictably condemned the "invasion", stating that more diplomatic means should have been employed.

A slightly wearied yet steadfast Sir Thomas Leese sat among his fellow national leaders of the U.L.D.N. at the large table within their holoconference.

ASCENSION

In accord with policy, and as a result of the multiple assassination event of Europe's leaders at the dawn of the Islamic Revolution, the members were not actually physically together at their bi-weekly meeting. Each sat in their respective capital, embattled from the past month's events, yet optimistic in looking to the possibilities ahead.

Sir Thomas was grateful, for the most part, in how things had turned out; though in some way he felt the weight of each life lost. What he had not anticipated, however, let alone authorized, was the final deal that was brokered between the Caliph Ali Bakr and none other than the Mystic King. In a private meeting, not more than a week into the battle, the Caliph had agreed to release his hold on Europe in exchange for free passage to Mecca, where he would be permitted to remain in power. By that point, amid heavy public pressure to "end the hostilities", Sir Thomas felt that he had no choice but to establish a corridor running through the former Slavic states and entering the former Turkey via Istanbul for the emigration of all Muslims who desired to remain with their Caliph.

The Caliph was subsequently able to consolidate his power within Arabia, Turkey, Iraq, and the entire remaining Middle East, minus Kurdistan and Israel, which were now both surrounded by hostile forces. Again, the Mystic King was able to ensure non-aggression towards these nations, at least at the hands of the newly established Arabian Empire. Sir Thomas felt at this juncture that he was powerless to invalidate this agreement, and the U.L.D N. nations, as well as the North American Union, quickly signed and ratified the accord. There would be no further incursion by the U.L.D.N. into the now sovereign Islamic Arabia.

Though perhaps a surprise to the Caliph (though not to Sir Thomas), the collapse of Eurabia sent all the remaining provinces of the Islamic Union into chaos, which encouraged subsequent invasions by opportunistic non-U.L.D.N. nations. The African Union, consisting of the sub-Saharan communist states, invaded the province of Northern Africa. The reconstituted Soviet Union (minus Russia, Lithuania, and Belarus) invaded the Islamic provinces of Iran and Afghanistan. The Chinese Empire moved its massive forces into the provinces of both Pakistan and Indonesia. Though the fighting would most likely continue in these areas for many months—if not even a year—it was evident at this point that each Islamic provincial government would eventually fall. The final Islamic province, however—the expanded Arabia—would be secure thanks to the actions of the Mystic King.

And today, as far as the world was concerned, Jimi T. Expo, not Sir Thomas Leese, was the hero of the moment, and its leaders would no doubt be looking to him to engage in dialogue with the remaining warring nations. Yet much to the chagrin of the Mystic King, and perhaps even in spite of him, Sir Thomas had independently authorized tens of thousands of Christian missionaries out of Russia—bishops, priests, and seminarians—to flood the spiritually devastated Europe. He was determined to provide the continent an opportunity to reclaim its Christian roots… if they so chose.

"I would like to thank each of you," Sir Thomas began, "for your support and sacrifice in the liberation of the continent of Europe. If for no other reason, the existence of the United League of Democratic Nations has been affirmed, and perhaps its greatest purpose has been fulfilled."

Each member of the League nodded in acknowledgement. For the most part, they appeared wearied, yet resolute in their commitment to press forward. Still, the fatalistic tone in their chairman's words did not escape them. Sir Thomas had only a week left of his time as Prime Minister of Great Britain, and three months remaining on his term as Chairman of the U.L.D.N. He had made it clear in no uncertain terms that he wished to step down at that point.

"It has been a difficult time, and I am certain there is much work ahead in rebuilding the infrastructure within Europe. Yet this victory has not been without unintended consequences… as is always the case with war."

"You speak of the establishment of the Islamic Arabian Empire?" It was Nikolai Petrov, Premier of Russia speaking. "Or perhaps the invasions of the remaining provinces of the Islamic Union? Or perhaps even, the unlikely ascension of Mr. Jimi T. Expo in the eyes of the world?"

A somewhat sad smile emerged from the countenance of Sir Thomas.

"I suppose all three to some degree or another. I do not want to diminish in any way that some good, albeit perhaps temporary, has come of this man's actions. Much bloodshed, at least in the short-term, has been averted. And further, I do not desire to question his motives either. Personally, it would have been my wish to make the Caliph answer for his crimes against humanity… but perhaps that will happen another day, and by another body."

"Another body?" Petrov inquired. All members of the League seemed to lean forward at this point.

"Yes," Sir Thomas responded, and after taking a deep breath, continued. "It is my belief that a more encompassing body… one to succeed the U.L.D.N., is inevitable. I say this with great apprehension, but President Maison of the North American Union is strongly pushing it, as are India, the socialist states of South America, and the Independent States of Scandinavia. I do not feel we can ignore their calls for long."

"These sorts of international bodies have consistently weakened national sovereignty in their tenures..." It was the President of Portugal, Francisco Jacintio, speaking this time. "Yet at the same time, they have all eventually been rendered innocuous, as collectively there seems never to be a common will among different peoples to address the true issues which affect our world. We have never been able to come to a shared agreement on what poses a threat, and what is a desirable vision of a unified planet."

Sir Thomas nodded. "I understand this. But work is underway by a growing consensus to establish such a body. The time is ripe, as they would say. I see that our choices are limited; we can either ignore this and potentially become an isolated—and even impotent—union, or we can place ourselves at the center of these negotiations, ensuring that we not only have a voice, but a strong one."

"And what of Israel, and the Vatican? Do you expect them to go along, Thomas?" It was the aging Tomasz Ian Dziwisz, Prime Minister of Poland speaking.

"They will have to make their own decisions as far as to what degree they desire to have involvement in the process, and even regarding their membership in this proposed body. Israel is surrounded by nations hostile to its existence." Then looking to the President of Honduras, Lempira Cortés, "As is Honduras. It would seem to be to each country's advantage to be involved. Yet all three seem to be carry the favor of the Almighty—a protection which I am afraid we could never aspire to match..."

iii

Siro sat in the front row of the greatly thinned press corps as the President of the United States—as well as Chairman of the North American Union—stepped to the podium. The closed session of Congress had been surprisingly brief. The gathering had been in direct response, Siro was certain, to the recently reported plot by a Christian religionist group to bomb the headquarters of The Way of Mystic Realism. The plot had been foiled due to the quick thinking of a *Rœbōi* named Nick Orieton. Six Christian extremists had been killed in the firefight that followed the botched operation, and a seventh was captured, fully confessing to the scheme. It was most likely the information gained from his interrogation that served as the catalyst for the president's meeting with Congress.

William Maison grasped both sides of the presidential podium, clearly grim faced.

"Good evening to all the citizens of the world. I come to you with very difficult news today, and in the direst of circumstances. As you know, we have striven to be an open-minded and tolerant nation, allowing people to live as they please so long as their lifestyles and beliefs brought harm to no one. Unfortunately, some have used this openness to advance their own ideologies, and have now evolved into the use of lethal force to impress their own beliefs on others, while violently suppressing those that do not share those beliefs.

"Last week, our administration was able to avert what would have been a major terrorist act on North American soil. With the subsequent capture of one of the Christian extremists, we learned under interrogation that this was not an isolated act but part of a much larger conspiracy by a group that refers to itself as the 'Christian Resistance'. Publicly, members of this group continue to insist they are a non-violent movement, but our investigation has indicated otherwise. We have learned that this plot—and others that are being planned—are widespread, including the participation of deacons, priests, and bishops, ascending to the highest levels of the Christian Church and the Vatican itself. As such, we recognize that this is not an act of domestic terrorism, but one of an organized foreign aggressor, with agents acting throughout our nation.

"In the face of this crisis, it is critical that we act swiftly, decisively, and courageously. We cannot let a misguided understanding of 'tolerance' prevent us from standing up against those forces who would oppose our liberty. Indeed, it was the Vatican itself who first fully demonstrated its intolerance by condemning The Way of Mystic Realism... which itself seeks only to embrace all people of all beliefs.

"So, in looking at the growing religionist antagonism towards our way of life, including the recent murder of a *Ræpōi* in Ohio, the assassination of President Hugh Lang, and of course, the dirty-bomb incident, which still is ingrained in our minds, an entire history of religionist aggression compels us today to say ... ENOUGH!"

Maison pounded his hand on the podium, causing everyone in attendance to momentarily jump. Yet not an instant later, all the president could see before him were unanimous nods of affirmation. He continued.

"It is with great regret that I have had to meet with Congress to put forth the following legislation and Executive Order; it is called the Freedom Against Intolerant Religion Act, or F.A.I.R. The primary initiatives of this act are as follows: One, all clergy of the major monotheistic religions, be they bishops, priests, deacons, rabbis, mullahs, and the like, will have seventy-two hours to renounce their offices and accept employment within the national workforce in an area deemed appropriate by the N.A.U. Labor Board. Some, of course, will not be willing to abide by this initiative. We have already spoken, just moments ago, with the President of Honduras, who is willing to accept anyone who falls under this category. As well, the Arabian Empire has offered to accept any Muslim leaders who wish to immigrate, and though there are few Jewish leaders remaining in our nation following the call home by the Nation of Israel, they too can emigrate to their country of origin. Any N.A.U. citizens from the previously referenced groups who choose to remain without renouncing their office will be considered enemies of the state and will be swiftly arrested."

Maison paused briefly. The nods of the press corps continued, even providing an impression of collective *relief.* He continued.

"Two, as of today, all property and other assets currently in possession of these religionist sects is to be annexed by the N.A.U. and speedily handed over to other non-ideological philanthropic organizations, such as Operation: Restore Spirit.

"Three, for those religionists who are non-leaders in their particular sect, their right to assemble for religionist purposes is suspended indefinitely, until we are able to navigate through this crisis."

With that the president and chairman halted, running his fingers through his hair, appearing sincerely distraught. "On a more personal note, I need to share how truly devastating this has been for me and my family. As a former permanent deacon in the Catholic Church, I had hoped that my faith tradition would grow beyond its narrow-minded past and embrace the reality that its time—at least in its current form—had passed. But instead of speaking words of love, hope, and openness, the Pope has put hundreds of millions at risk by clinging to an antiquated belief system. I can only hope that Christians will recognize their leadership for what it is, and be an authentic voice for the faithful in promoting true change from within."

4

The Signs of the Times

The Signs of the Times ح
<<n 2.210>>

LONDON, Great Britain - Now in the third month of what some have dubbed "World War III", the call for a global body to broker a diplomatic resolution to the series of armed conflicts has reached its apex. Despite the temporary absence of aggression in Europe, fighting within North Africa, Iran, Afghanistan, Pakistan, and Indonesia continues to rage on with the loss of innocent life reaching Biblical proportions. Experts are in agreement that, without immediate intervention on a global level, a nuclear exchange is inevitable.

Jimi T. Expo, who negotiated the peaceful handover of Eurabia to invading U.L.D.N. forces, has stepped forward with a proposal for a new international body, which currently has the backing of the North American Union, the Independent Scandinavian States, the South American Socialist Union, India, and the Soviet Union. In an encouraging recent communication, the United League of Democratic Nations has stated that the association is "open" to the new body under certain still undisclosed conditions. Sources within the African Union and the Chinese Empire have also indicated a "newfound openness" to the proposal by their nations, perhaps due to a growing weariness with the ongoing bloodshed resulting from their respective invasions.

To date, the only major political power that staunchly opposes the proposed international body, currently dubbed "The Global Communion", is the Arabian Empire. It is unclear at this time whether this would pose an insurmountable obstacle to the establishment of the international body.

ASCENSION

i

Father Daniel had spent the past three days in prayer and fasting, with Brother Hanoch faithfully interceding alongside of him. During this time, they continued to petition for clarity as to what God was asking of them; entreating for even the slightest illumination as to His will at this juncture. It seemed that every step taken brought them to another crossroads revealing multiple paths, none of which offered a clear black or white choice.

As the pair completed a private Mass over which Father Daniel presided, they remained kneeling in prayer, savoring their experience of communion at its deepest and most intimate levels with their Sovereign Redeemer.

Father Daniel felt the maternal presence return, more powerfully than she had in many years. The presence had consistently provided him much-needed consolation, yet he always knew that she came with a more solemn purpose—a task that he could freely accept or allow to pass. Nevertheless, at this point in his faith journey, he could not imagine denying any request given to him from above. Too much... too *many*... rested in the balance.

Sensing the transcending moment, Hanoch placed his hand on Father Daniel's shoulder. The fullness of the presence enveloped the priest, and he collapsed to the floor.

It was shortly thereafter that Father Daniel awoke, retaining no memory of anything—save the maternal presence—that had occurred while he rested in the Spirit.

"Your destined path has come into focus," Hanoch stated as he helped Father Daniel rise to a sitting position in the pew.

Father Daniel, feeling peaceful yet invigorated, nodded soberly. His companion waited a moment longer before speaking again.

"Father, the time is growing short. The final act of the Elect on this Earth is rapidly approaching—the time for 'The Gathering' is near. You have been faithful to God's calling on your life... especially in your intercession."

The priest looked serenely at Hanoch, nodding in acknowledgement. "There are still those I pray for that I do not know... their names too were inscribed on the chalice in the vision from years ago."

Hanoch provided a temperate nod of acknowledgement. "It may not be His will that you have personal knowledge of each soul... only that you are called to intercede on their behalf. You still have work left to do in aid of those whom the Lord has revealed your call to pastor. Yet your final task on this Earth has now been brought to light."

Father Daniel looked into Hanoch's eyes of ageless wisdom, pieces of a dream starting to reassemble in his mind. Revelation suddenly pierced his thoughts.

"How can this be asked of me?" he inquired, feeling the icy fingers of doubt begin to enter his spirit. "Is there even the most remote chance of success?"

Hanoch gazed steadily at the priest. "Success can have a very elusive meaning and form. But a choice must always be offered. *All* have been created with the Kingdom as their final destiny, yet not all choose this path."

"And if I fail?"

"You have your part to play, yet ultimately it will not be *your* success... nor *your* failure. Conversion is an act of the Holy Spirit, but the soul *must* freely respond to the grace offered. It is that response that makes all the difference; the choice remains."

"I must do this alone?"

"A cloud of witnesses will surround you."

ASCENSION

ii

"Thomas, I would humbly request that you reconsider. It disturbs me to no minor degree thinking of who would serve in the capacity of Sovereign of the Global Communion should you not accept."

Sir Thomas Leese, speaking from his small vacation (and soon to be *retirement*) cottage in Blackrock, Ireland, shook his head at the image of his Russian friend, Nikolai Petrov, on the holoconference.

"Nikolai, I have served my time, I am growing older and wearier. I desire a quiet retirement, and to only become a better parent to Adam."

The premier nodded in acknowledgement. "I do understand, my friend, believe me when I say that. Family comes first, of that there is no question. But as sovereign, the way this body has been arranged, you would only need to be available via holoconference for one two-hour meeting each week, and then a three-day conference at one of the twelve undisclosed locations once a quarter. The rest you can delegate and assign to committees."

Sir Thomas again shook his head as he leaned back in his seat and rubbed his fatigued eyes. "Even the name, 'Sovereign', it just drips with connotations that I do not wish to even enter into. I have never been an advocate of a single governing body in the world. I understand and in some ways even concede its inevitability—I acknowledge no less before the U.L.D.N. But I feel it weakens individual nations and kills culture."

"Yet perhaps, under your leadership," Petrov persisted, "it could be different. You could fulfill John Paul II's optimistic hopes for the United Nations; a respecter of cultures, supporter of the poor and oppressed, and a staunch force against aggressors."

Sir Thomas stared off into nothingness, a dreamy expression resting on his face. "What I would do for a dose of his optimism right now. I'm afraid my experience in life has not led me to a certain belief in the goodness of man." Then, turning his gaze back to Petrov he added, "I even see things that disquiet me in my own nephew. Adam is a good boy, but I see a restlessness within him that he does not permit me to channel and guide."

"Such is the life of a father. And tell me, what does young Adam think about you accepting the position?"

"Well, since his hero the Mystic King is advocating my service, the lad is all for it."

The Russian premier paused at this point. "You know, Thomas, I would be the first to say that this man's belief system is far from yours or mine. But I cannot help but acknowledge the fact that he has done some good. As we speak, it seems as if he is going to be able to broker similar agreements in the remaining countries of the old Islamic Union... permitting their Islamic leaders and all followers who wish to have free passage to a final 'exile' in Arabia, while allowing their former countries to be absorbed into the North African Union, the Soviet Union, and the Chinese Empire. Perhaps we have been a bit hasty in judging the man."

Sir Thomas had to admit that in moments of weakness he held doubts himself of his own position on Jimi T. Expo. The enigmatic man *had* done good, and despite Sir Thomas' unsuccessful attempts to block Operation: Restore Spirit from entry into liberated Europe, it had had unprecedented success in promoting civil tranquility throughout the cities of the Old Continent in only a few short months. Still, this man believed things which Sir Thomas found to be irreconcilable with his own understanding of the human person... and throughout the history of humanity, these faulty beliefs had always led to totalitarianism and even genocide. Could it really be possible that this time it could be different?

"Thomas?"

Sir Thomas broke himself from his brief reverie. "Yes? Oh... I'm sorry... this is just so much. And really, if Mr. Expo truly wanted the Arabian Empire to join this Global Communion, the last person he would want to lead this body would be... what do they call me... the 'Genocidal Spawn of Satan?'"

Petrov released a guarded chuckle, yet he did not directly respond. "It is my understanding that even our reigning Pope has contacted you on this matter."

Sir Thomas sighed. "Yes, and he too encouraged me to accept the post... with certain caveats of course."

"So then, what more do you require?"

Sir Thomas looked directly at the holo-image of his friend, speaking with conviction. "Will all parties agree to acknowledge in the preamble of the organizing charter that our rights come from God and not man?"

"We have, with Mr. Expo's assistance, been able to reach a compromise that permits a statement to be made in reference to a 'higher power'."

Sir Thomas shook his head. "I suppose that is as much as I could have hoped for. You believe all national unions will come on board then?"

ASCENSION

"I think there is a good possibility that all but Arabia will. But just between you and me, Thomas, if you do *not* accept this position, I do not believe this body stands a chance of lasting more than a year, and in my estimation, we will not get another shot for at least a generation, and only after much greater world crises have taken their course. So I ask you, Sir Thomas... for the sake of humanity... will you accept?"

iii

"I have sensed this coming for some time, and the stars state that the timing is right," Madame Opfree proclaimed.

Sister Sawlus nodded in agreement. Yet even if she had not agreed with the statement, she would still have nodded. Arguing with one's personal psychic would be purely ridiculous.

"This Mystic King is like no other," Sawlus replied.

Opfree smiled intensely. Her smooth dark skin defied a true portrayal of her many years, and her intense eyes, one blue and the other green, completed her inscrutable presence; this woman was anything but ordinary. "He is none less than the promised Messiah, my precious. It is only through him that we might be saved."

Some within The Way had expressed concern over Jimi T.'s transition from musician/philanthropist into the political arena. Then again, these skeptics would have to acknowledge that he had never sought a political position. Yet, with his ascension to his first political post, and his resolution of the Eurabian conflict, the Mystic King had made the transition seem like the most natural event that had ever occurred in the history of mankind.

"The concept of separation of Spirit and State is a fallacy that, through the love of the Spiritual Entity, never was able to fully become established in our hearts," he had stated. *"Any true political, social, or economic entity springs forth from its relationship to the* Kôles, *without which it would be doomed to failure."*

"It is true..." Opfree remarked, waking Sawlus from her daydream. "That which claims to be not of the *Kôles* is not of the body and must be cut off!"

"Praised be the Spirit," Sawlus replied, quickly remembering Opfree's keen powers of mind reading. "So you see good things for the proposed Global Communion?"

"I do, Sister, though I foresee its genesis being one of great turmoil."

Sawlus had been no less than ecstatic when, after only four months in politics, the Mystic King stood—curiously, without the Great Prophet at his side—and proposed the establishment of the Global Communion. It was a simplistic proposal really. Eliminate representatives and have the head of each nation sit on the council. The head, called the "Sovereign", would renounce his or her national citizenship to truly serve as a global citizen, agreeing never to return to his or her country of origin for life. At this point, all of the major national unions had accepted membership… all but one that is.

"And what of the Arabian Empire, Madame Opfree?" she asked.

Opfree closed her eyes briefly, then opened them, seemingly gazing right through her client. "I have looked into this deeply. The Mystic King will persuade its leaders to embrace the new Communion, and it will then serve as the uniting force to bring us all together."

Sawlus felt relieved. She knew that the Arabian Empire had held out due to the fact that the greatest proponent of The Way of Mystic Realism had proposed the plan. But certainly even more so because the man singly responsible for the deaths of over one million of their fellow religionists had been proposed as its head. Yet in truth, Sawlus had no doubt that The Way was the reason the G.C. was so quickly ratified by all the participating national unions, and Leese… well… he was still popular internationally. Perhaps he would be a necessary evil to get the Global Communion on its feet?

Still, from Sawlus' perspective, Israel was the real kicker; though a choosing the role of a non-member state, they had immediately ratified the entity's Charter. Sawlus would have sworn that Israel, a land under the control of the *Ďishalâk*, would not accept this proposal. Though the appointment of Eliot Kohein Lige as their ambassador to the body (the non-member states were not permitted to be represented by their heads) did make Sawlus a tad anxious. It was rumored that this particular appointment was a non-negotiable stipulation of Leese before his consideration of his own position in the entity.

"It is true, these people have unwarranted faith in this man called Leese," Opfree stated, again reading Sawlus' thoughts.

"And what of this man?" Sawlus inquired. "He is not of The Way."

Opfree nodded slowly. "This is true, but he is playing an integral part in the Great Plan, and it will not be long before he comes to know the true path of the *Kôles*."

Sawlus smiled in delight. "Then he will be one with us?"

Opfree nodded, though perhaps not as affirmatively as Sawlus would have hoped.

Indeed, Sawlus' greatest fear was that the Global Communion, though proposed by Jimi T. Expo, was to be headed by a Christian. But the U.L.D.N. member-states, Scandinavia, and India, as well as the three non-member states, refused ratification if Leese was not to be its first sovereign. And after all that, the gall of the Christian, he had to be heavily persuaded by the Pope himself to accept the reins.

Sawlus scribbled down every bit of information she could, then casually slipped into the part of the session she was most interested in.

"So, Madame Opfree, what do you see in the future for me and my son?"

"Oh, my dear, I see a wonderful year ahead for young Caleb. He will do us all proud."

Sawlus beamed. "And me?"

Opfree rhythmically moved her hands along her crystals, maintaining a serene look upon her countenance. However, a sudden flash of... of... *pain?* swept across her face. It was gone in a moment but had been sustained long enough for Sawlus to notice.

"What is it, Madame? Was did you see? Was it something bad?"

Opfree opened her eyes and shook her head with a maternal smile. "No, my dear, I am sorry. It is just that I have developed a splitting headache, and it is partially blocking my passageway to the *Kôles*."

"Oh, here, let me get you some *Cimä*," Sawlus insisted as she began to fumble through her purse.

Opfree shook her head apologetically and held up her hand. "Oh, no, my dear. It is quite all right. Perhaps I just need a bit of rest. We can reschedule, yes?"

Sawlus stopped, unable to mask her sense of disappointment. "We... sure, I guess we can do that."

"Fine, then," Opfree responded, still not appearing to be her usual self.

After a brief moment of scrutiny, Sawlus reached over and placed her palm onto the fiscal reader. A tone sounded, and she then punched in the charge for the session, along with her usual generous tip.

She really was grateful of Opfree, who had always helped her get the lead and inside scoop on any story. And Opfree, who used to read palms on a side store in an alleyway in Louisiana, now saw only select clients at her multimillion-dollar estate.

"The *Neöret* has been good to you, Madame Opfree," Sawlus remarked as she rose and reached for her purse.

Opfree nodded slowly and smiled. "It has been good to all those who preserve an open mind."

Sawlus was about to turn to leave when her eyes caught a single framed photograph resting on the bookcase behind Opfree. It was of a boy in perhaps his late teens, his skin tone reflecting some degree of African-American descent, though clearly he was biracial. Yet what drew her attention the most were the stunning emerald green eyes. Something within her spirit moved—like an exceptional sense of déjà vu.

"That picture… that boy…"

Madame Opfree turned only partway towards the bookcase, then returned her gaze to Sawlus, her eyes narrowing slightly.

"That is my son."

Sawlus could not shake the disconcerting feeling within her, but it was clear that this was not a topic upon which her personal psychic wished to elaborate. Sawlus shook her head as if to clear her mind. "I'm sorry. He is a very… attractive young man. I'm sure he has made you very proud. Until next time?"

Opfree nodded, and Sawlus turned and slipped out the door.

Opfree remained staring at the door for some time, contemplating many thoughts within her. She began humming a tune which caused the many crystals in her shop to shimmer.

"Dere be much in your days ahead dat is shrouded, woman," she whispered. "You best be takin' care wit de tings you got commin', dat is for sure."

iv

"The answer is no… you *cannot* have tomorrow off. Really, Ms. Nesterov, you only have to work three six-hour shifts a week, and you *still* ask for more time off? You're just as lazy as the rest of these deadbeats around here."

Annie D. was certainly not accustomed to being spoken to in this way, yet she calmly swallowed her pride as her nurse-in-charge, Kate Thomas, continued to rant. It was moments such as these that caused her to question her decision to stay in Philadelphia, not accepting Father Daniel's invitation to serve with him in upstate New York. Yet, in the end, she had the sense that things for her were still not finished here.

"All you people... you get your high-falutin' government check in the mail, and you think you don't even have to work anymore. Well, I've got news for you, missy, we *all* have to work—it's the law. A lot of these parasites are going to be sorry when I report them to the N.A.U. Labor Board!"

"If you please," Annie D. began, trying to be firm yet respectful. "I'm only askin' for a day, nothin' more. It's Sunday, and though the law forbids our gatherin' for the Mass, I can still honor me Lord with a day of rest and prayer in His name."

"Sunday? Are you living in a cave? There *are* no more Sundays. We have a six-day week now... five six-day weeks make a month, twelve thirty-day months make a year. Add to that the celebration of the *Kat'häl*, and you have a full cycle... why is that too difficult to get into your skull?"

Annie D. persisted. "Aye, I'm fully realizin' the government... well, perhaps *most* governments have taken on this novelty of a calendar. But I've been trackin' the days meself. Tomorrow is the Lord's Day."

Nurse Thomas sneered. "You sicken me, you know that? You still want to live in a decaying sect that does nothing but judge that everything anyone else does is *evil*. I'd have thought with all of your priests expelled throughout the Union, you'd have come to your senses."

"Aye, Ms. Thomas, and we'll rue the day for permittin' such a thing! Yet we still have our deacons, thank the good Lord, and we're abidin' by the law, though it's unjust."

"The 'good Lord'? No... you thank the Mystic King. His intervention on your behalf to allow this exception... it is beyond any mercy your kind deserves. Too generous—that's what I think our leaders are being. I wish you would all have one big final powwow together, and that one merciful soul would drop the big one on you and put you all out of your misery—and put us out of ours."

Annie D. sighed. "Aye, Nurse Thomas. Sadly, you may one day be gettin' your wish."

5

To: **Sir Thomas Leese, Sovereign-Nominee, Global Communion**

From: **Joran Waddock, Chief of Staff**

Date: **February 11 (n. 2.266)**

Re: **Summary of critical articles of G.C. Constitution**

Sir Thomas:

Per your request, our team has poured over this 451-page document of the new Global Communion. This is an initial Executive Summary of the most critical points, followed by a more detailed twelve-page summary of all articles and sections.

 † Per your demand, the preamble clearly identifies the rights of persons to come from a "higher power", and not man.

 † The G.C. consists of the head of state of the following nations/national unions: The U.L.D.N. (including Europe), African Union, North American Union, South American Socialist Union, Chinese Empire, India, Soviet Union, and Independent Scandinavian States. It now appears that the Arabian Empire will also join. For the initial three years of the G.C., each member-state of the former U.L.D.N., including Kurdistan, will have 1/3 vote in all matters, At the end of this period, the collective former-U.L.D.N. nations will essentially function as a single national union, possessing one vote. At this time, there will also be the option for a scheduled global referendum, potentially re-aligning national union boundaries and membership statuses.

 † Three nation-states have accepted non-member status: Israel, Honduras, and the Vatican State. Per statute, their heads of state do not participate, only appointed ambassadors. They cannot vote in any G.C. matters, yet have a prescribed time for stating their position on any issue that is brought to a vote.

 † The governing individual of the G.C. carries the title of "Sovereign", and is elected by a simple majority of the voting members of the G.C. He/She must immediately relinquish his/her citizenship to his/her country of origin, and agree never to return, even after his/her seven-year term is completed. Once elected, his/her country of origin of course must elect a new head of state. However, to avoid undue influence (with the Sovereign being a former member of that country as well, and still most likely have loyalties therein), the *deputy* head of the Sovereign's former nation-state will then serve on the G.C., as opposed to the head.

 † In addition to the heads of the member states, one curious statute permits up to three "special envoys" to sit on the G.C. as voting members. These envoys must be nominated by a member state other than their own, and then be ratified by a super-majority of the G.C. As with the Sovereign, they too must then relinquish their citizenship of their country of origin. After their ratification, they have full rights on the G.C., and can even serve as acting Sovereign for up to a three-year period in a situation of "global crisis." The statute does not specifically identify what constitutes a crisis, only that a 2/3 majority must agree to it.

 † The G.C. convenes once a week by holoconference on Monday at twelve noon G.S.T. for two hours. All the rest of the work and meetings are done at subordinate levels. Once a quarter, the G.C. meets at one of twelve reserved, remote locations. It will not be publicly disclosed as to *which* of these locations is being utilized, for obvious security reasons. A quite intricate system has been established that provides a number of decoys in travel so as not to allow individuals to be tracked. Of note, these twelve locations will serve as the "residences" of the Sovereign as well, and though he/she is permitted to travel, as aforementioned, he/she cannot return to his/her country of origin.

ASCENSION

i

"So the Arabian Empire has agreed to join the Global Communion?" Eliot Kohein Lige, newly appointed ambassador of non-member State of Israel to the G.C., inquired.

"Yes, my friend, they have," Sovereign Thomas Leese responded almost indifferently.

Eli looked at him curiously. "What is it, Thomas?"

Sir Thomas turned his wheelchair and moved towards the window. He had reluctantly made the decision to accept the request to serve as Sovereign of the G.C., and in exchange for his service, he had given up his citizenship of Great Britain.

I will never again be able to set foot on the soil of my homeland.

Surely, he now had a residence to call his own on each of twelve secret island locations across the globe. Though despite this, he felt like someone who had no place to lay their head. This first meeting of the Global Communion was taking place at G.C. One in the south pacific.

"Thomas?"

He had drifted off again. Despite his assurances to the contrary to his nephew, it *was* becoming more common. Sir Thomas was feeling every one of his sixty-one years. His thoughts would move towards his spouse of only nine months, the son he never met, his slain sister and brother-in-law, Adam, who, though excited about his uncle's position, did not altogether like the idea of not being able to return to his homeland until he was a man himself.

"Thomas?"

Sir Thomas regathered himself and looked back to Eli. "The Arabs... the Muslims... their condition on joining was that Jimi T. Expo be named Special Envoy to the Communion."

Eli looked up at his new friend, unable to mask his dismay. "*What? That is beyond odd.*" He paused for a moment, reflecting on what process would have brought this unlikely demand to fruition. "The Islamic leaders have been disparaging Mystic Realism all along—truly, it too is incompatible with Islam. But this? I do not see how we can permit it."

Sir Thomas turned back at him and shook his head. "We cannot prevent it. I have already received transmittals that seven of the eight primary member-states have accepted this proposal, and for some inexplicable reason, Kurdistan has cast their one-third vote in favor. That's the two-thirds super-majority required."

Eli maintained a steady gaze and paused a moment before speaking. "I suppose this should not surprise us. The enemies of *Elohim* are many. Whether they knowingly conspire against His plan, or are simply pawns of His adversary, we must stand firm... we must, no matter what comes against us, be willing to fight the good fight."

"What can be done, then... I mean, realistically?" Sir Thomas inquired with an uncharacteristically despondent tone. "It is clear now that there has been collusion behind the scenes in the establishment of this body. Special envoys are granted some significant powers within the G.C.—for which I will need to scour the Charter to be certain as to where those powers begin and end." He hesitated for a moment, pondering another thought. "However, it is more the unofficial influence that this man carries that concerns me. I wonder if words on paper will restrain him."

Eli paused momentarily, further pondering this unanticipated occurrence before standing. An expression of resolution, even hope, emerged upon his countenance.

"We have not lost in any sense of the word, Thomas. We must trust that, if *Elohim* has permitted this, we will be able to endure it. Despite my nation's non-voting status, I will support you all the way in there, my friend. We still hold the reins... and *Elohim* is truly still... Sovereign."

Sir Thomas sat up in his wheelchair, moving back towards Eli, a bit discomfited by his momentary lack of faith. "And I am with you, my friend. Until whatever conclusion God sees fit to bring upon us."

They shook hands and then embraced. A buzz came from the intercom.

"Yes, yes, Joran," Sir Thomas remarked. "I am aware that it is time for the Council to convene."

A voice chirped back. "Yes, sir, but it's just that there is someone here who wishes to see you before the meeting."

Sir Thomas scowled. "What do you mean, someone—?"

"Good day, Sovereign."

ASCENSION

Both Sir Thomas and Eli jerked their heads to the west entrance of the office. There stood the man about whom they had been speaking.

A slight smile emerged from the Mystic King's face. "Do you not think it appropriate that we speak before the first Council convenes, Sovereign?" And with a slight cocking of the head, perhaps acknowledging Eli, he added, "Alone..."

ii

"I do not know how much longer we are going to permit this to continue!"

As Luther, a.k.a. Tæsír Hoc, a.k.a. the Great Prophet stood before the *Illumini*, it was clear that he was infuriated to the point of losing control.

"Really, Luther," the one called Marius intoned darkly. "It is not as if he is just another sideshow leader to our cause... he is the Anointed!"

"You would have me begin to believe," Luther retorted, seething, "that your time in Jerusalem has clouded your mind, Marius."

But Marius could not restrain his own grin. "Perhaps, but what is it that he has done that has you so... *incensed?*"

Luther looked out across the twenty-member group. He was the last... he was the one to usher in the age of their own promised Messiah. And it was he himself that had first guided the one who was to become the Mystic King. Yet he found himself being condescended to at every juncture, and he was no longer even consulted on major decisions. It was as if something had changed in the man he once called...

"Luther?"

He looked back to Marius, responding with his growing sense of disgust. "Is it not apparent to all of you? He is clearly attempting to bring order where we have attempted to sow chaos. He is giving hope, when we desire to foment despair. It seems even The Way has fallen to an afterthought, subjugated to his precious 'Operation' and now this foolish 'Global Communion.' And did he not persuade Brother William to amend a beautifully crafted legislative act so that Christians are permitted to assemble, albeit in private residences, and that their deacons may remain in-country? This is insanity! He has become too political... too populist... he has forgotten the face of his father!"

"Yet, as brother Marius has pointed out," Cato interjected, "he is not simply one of our pawns which we can use today and dispense with tomorrow. He is the Anointed One. He has been chosen—"

"I TOO HAVE BEEN CHOSEN!"

The outburst was a surprise to even this shadowed council, and the room grew suddenly cold and dark, save the light luminescence emanating from its members.

A somewhat subdued Cato was the first to speak, though still not without a hint of sarcasm in his voice. "Do you suggest, then, Luther, that the Master has made a mistake?"

"I do not..." Luther responded, beginning to compose himself. "Only that the 'Anointed' seems to be serving his own agenda rather than fully aligning himself with the Master's plan."

"Are you certain that it is not you, Luther, who is perhaps not willing to accept your subordinate role to the Anointed?"

Luther sneered. "My only interest, Eumenes, is in the Master's plan, and fulfilling my part in it."

There was a communal reflective pause amongst the dark coterie lasting no more than a few moments.

"We are listening," Anaxagoras spoke, encouraging Luther to proceed. "What is it that you propose?"

This was more like it. He did not necessarily have their hearts, but at least for the moment, he had their ears.

"I propose only that we do not allow ourselves to be spellbound by his many manipulations. We support those initiatives which are aligned with the Master's ageless plan, and undermine those which would draw these stupid monkeys out of their personal cesspools of self-absorbed mediocrity."

iii

Sister Sawlus and Siro Scribner lay in bed, awaking to a beautiful day. Caleb still lay asleep in the next room. They gazed out across the breathtaking scenery of the Mediterranean

"I think I'd prefer the Caribbean to be honest, Siro."

"So be it…" Siro spoke confidently. "Change scene… Caribbean as viewed from St. Thomas."

Instantly the scene changed to a beautiful deep blue sea. Sawlus smiled. It was the first time they had been together in several months… both having incredibly busy schedules.

"So tell me, my love, what is your latest scoop?"

Siro shrugged as he reached for his coffee on the nightstand. "Nothing very exciting. It seems that twenty million Christians from the North American Union have accepted the offer made by Honduras. The Kurds, of all people, have facilitated the process. It's being kept publicly low key, but the final transport ships departed ten days ago. For whatever reason, Maison chose to provide as little public information as possible…even to Honduras. He just told them to make their ports available for whatever transports showed up. Really, I'm not sure how their economy will sustain them all."

"Good riddance, I say. Just think, Siro, a nation free of that scourge!"

Siro nodded, though he always felt a little uncomfortable when his *breha* spoke so virulently against anyone… even Christians. He himself had been a nominal Christian at one time, and it really wasn't his fault, he was just raised that way.

"Well, it isn't only those twenty million, it's estimated another ten million from our Union have also emigrated to other U.L.D.N. nations. It's really quite stunning what they've pulled off in a mere six weeks."

"And what does that leave here?"

"It is really hard to say… probably those who were more Christian in name or tradition, which we estimate to be about fifty million or so, have just found a good excuse to give it up. They were really there already, I mean, not truly practicing their religion, the F.A.I.R. Act has just caused them to be more honest about where they stood."

"Then that's it?"

"No, not hardly. It's believed there may still be as many as ten million in the U.S. alone who have gone underground… priests and even bishops. It appears Maison is going to establish a task force to root them out."

"That is just beautiful," Sawlus responded in an unnervingly sincere tone. "It's really happening, Siro, really. We will be able to raise Caleb, and our other children, in a liberated world free of hate."

Siro paused for a moment as what Sawlus had shared sunk in.

"Other children?"

6

His station is there;--and he works on the crowd,
He sways them with harmony merry and loud;
He fills with his power all their hearts to the brim--
Was aught ever heard like his fiddle and him!

What an eager assembly! what an empire is this!
The weary have life and the hungry have bliss;
The mourner is cheared, and the anxious have rest;
And the guilt-burthened Soul is no longer opprest.

> – William Wordsworth
> *The Power of Music*

i

The crowd roared, the band played, and the spirit of the *Kôles* filled the domed stadium. The forty-concert reunion tour had been put together in celebration of the tentative peace agreement recently established among the nine superpowers of the world. The temporary pact had been brokered by none other than the Mystic King, with a rumored "final solution" in the works that would provide the necessary components for a lasting world peace. The tour was intended to draw widespread support for the pact among the masses. This would be the final encore of *Çön Razón*, and the night could not have been more magical.

There had curiously been little spoken throughout the tour about the newly transformed zombie-man playing lead guitar. Certainly, he bore the likeness of Nathaniel Freeman-Page, played guitar the same, and even carried the same name, but that was where the similarities ended.

DOMINION

Nathaniel had given up on his fight to maintain dominion over his own personal existence. One moment he was free falling towards a death he had grown to crave, the next he found himself at the feet of the Mystic King. This final tour had been a blur to him amidst a slew of concerts and heavy doses of *Cimä*, but Jimi T. had kept the automaton called Nathaniel close by his side throughout.

He had finally gotten what he wanted out of this whole deal…

…the friendship of the Mystic King.

Yet it was only beginning to become clear to Nathaniel what further concessions he had made in order to achieve this goal.

"Before we say goodbye to you all," the Mystic King boomed to the enraptured throng, "we have one last piece to close with."

The crowd hushed to a deafening silence and listened for the Mystic King's final words to them in this capacity. No future tours were to become manifest. The work of *Çön Razón* had been consummated.

"The world is quickening in its transformation. Mankind has finally allowed the Spirit of the *Kôles* to flow freely within all that may seek Her, and we have moved to a new level of tranquility and happiness. Truly… change has come to our world!"

The crowd again roared, though quickly silenced, sensing there was yet more to be said.

"No man can question your good works, or the honorable intentions of the Spirit. Look around you and see; the chaos in the world is beginning to dissipate, and a new world order is emerging, one that does not depend on belief in a vengeful deity, but that understands the truths of our common existence." He paused for a moment, allowing the throng to absorb every word, then he continued in a more subdued tone. "Yet, truth be known, there are still those who still seek to condemn us."

The crowd gasped. Shouts of "No!" and "We're with you, Jimi," arose from the milieu.

The Mystic King held his hand up in acknowledgement of their cries yet commanding silence. "Yes, it is true. There are those who search for a dark side to the goodness that The Way has brought to our society. There are those who still have not outgrown the myths of old. Still, we must have compassion on these souls… for most, it is not their own fault that they have been led astray."

A complete and utterly focused energy encompassed all in attendance.

ASCENSION

"It is time for all of us to stop quarreling and love each other as the Spirit and I have loved you…"

The crowd roared again, both men and women cried tears of sadness and joy. This was a pure, self-fulfilling love that had been given as a gift to them by the New Messiah. Why could others not see that?

"So we leave you with this, and may the Spirit continue to abide within you."

And with that, the Mystic King looked over to Nathaniel, giving him a gentle and affectionate nod. A light, dreamy smile came to Nathaniel's face as he began to play.

A tune arose which was vaguely recognizable to some of the aged members of the audience. A familiar tune with a twist of the *Hôlmüs*. Then the haunting melodic voice chimed in…

> *Now I've been happy lately,*
> *Thinking about the good things to come,*
> *And I believe it could be*
> *Something good has begun.*
>
> *Now I've been smiling lately,*
> *Dreaming about the world as one*
> *And I believe it could be*
> *Something good's bound to come.*
>
> *'Cause out on the edge of darkness*
> *There rides the Peace Train*
> *Oh Peace Train, take this country*
> *Come take me home again…*

ii

Pope Peter peered out the window of his apartment overlooking Saint Peter's Square. Since his return just before the collapse of Eurabia, he had never ceased expressing gratitude to God for his homecoming. In the midst of his current moment of thankfulness, he absently allowed his hand to move towards his right side, where now two dozen of the sores had manifested themselves. The spread of the mysterious disease was indeed slow, yet it was steadily progressing. For now, he would keep the ailment to himself. God's means for bringing about His will were not always readily clear—nor easy for that matter—though their purpose was always certain.

From behind him, there was a knock at the door.

"Please come in."

Msgr. Craig Ebright entered the room.

"Holy Father, you wished to see me?"

The Pontiff turned and nodded, taking his hand from his side and clasping it with the other. "Yes, but I was hoping our two friends would be here to join us. Let's go into my study, and we will pray for a time before they arrive."

The pair opened the door to the Pope's private study, and there sitting at the large central table were Brother Eli and Brother Hanoch.

"Forgive me," the mildly surprised Pontiff exclaimed. "I did not realize you had arrived."

Each smiled, and Hanoch spoke. "We have found that it is much easier to get into places than out."

Peter and Msgr. Ebright each took seats at the table, and following a brief prayer the Pontiff addressed Eli and Hanoch. "I understand that you believe you have located the American priest of whom I have had the vision."

Eli nodded. "We believe so. His name is Father Daniel Ananias. He was originally the rector of the Cathedral in Philadelphia, but he is now in hiding in upstate New York. He is actually a Kurd by birth."

"A Kurd?" the Pontiff cocked an eyebrow. "That is quite an interesting patrimony—quite a... *providential* lineage."

Both Eli and Hanoch nodded in agreement. "This is true. We have found him to be devout and single-hearted. Our Lady has had her mantle of protection about him for some time. For these reasons, we believe he is the one of whom you have dreamed."

"Holy Father, if I may," Msgr. Ebright interjected. It was uncharacteristic of him to interrupt.

"Yes, Monsignor?"

"This Father Ananias, I believe I have met him. My brother served under him as a deacon in the Archdiocese of Philadelphia. He spoke quite highly of the man."

With that, Hanoch handed the pontiff a picture of Father Daniel. Peter nodded in the affirmative. "Yes, it is him... though in truth, I was certain of it before you even showed me this picture. Does he understand what is to be asked of him... his calling?"

"I believe so," Eli intimated. "Brother Hanoch has spent considerable time with him recently and has broached the subject, yet not in detail. To be clear, Holy Father, even we are not certain of the details of this mission."

"I understand. Though his day, as is mine, is approaching, I sense that we have a brief season before the designated time. Perhaps a few months, perhaps even a year, as best as I can foresee. But if Providence presents itself, I would wish to pray with him before the... confrontation. At that time, I do believe that your time to witness will be at hand."

Both Eli and Hanoch nodded solemnly, yet not without evidence of anticipation. "So be it, Holy Father. Shall we then set out to recover the Old Covenant?"

The Pontiff nodded. "Yes, it is time. Once obtained, place it in ancient Edom until the appointed time, and may God have mercy on us all."

The entire room remained silent as each man breathed his own prayer for strength in the time that was to come.

iii

"So tell me, Dr. Sanger, you feel you have made a breakthrough with my request?"

"I believe so... in fact, I am certain of it."

"Go on then, explain it to me."

It had pleased Dr. Mengel Sanger that he had once again ascended to the good graces of his long-time benefactor, Luther—now known to the world as the Great Prophet Tæsír Hoc. Following his development of *Cimä*, Sanger was wealthy beyond all comprehension, but for the most part, he was yesterday's news. He needed something new—something that would cause others to describe him, once again, as "brilliant."

He began his exposition. "Well, it is actually broken down into a process with three stages. In the first stage, a toxin is released. It is very much like a nerve gas, only more concentrated, and per your request, slow and progressive in its activation. It begins by heightening sensitivity to pain through the eradication of the nervous system's pain reducing functionality. Slowly, the nerve agent begins to intensify the pain, which after thirty minutes or so becomes quite excruciating."

"You have tested this on subjects, I take it?"

"Yes, I have, and to be honest, it has been difficult to find any who have lasted until the third stage. When we initiate the second stage, which I call E.S.R. - early selective reduction, via cessation instruments, most opt out of the experiment."

The Prophet looked annoyed. "Doctor, you have a penchant for providing complex descriptions for very simple matters. Are you trying to say that in the second stage you provide them the means to kill themselves, and they do?"

Sanger clearly recognized the admonishment. "Ahh... yes, my lord, that is what I am saying."

"Then say just that. Your fancy terminology irritates, not impresses."

"Yes, my lord."

"So what weapons do you provide them?"

"Guns and knives."

"Very well... the third stage, then... for those who somehow endure the physical pain and do not, 'opt out' as you say?"

"Well, the nerve gas also has another compound in it that is quite amazing. The long and the short of it is that this compound targets the portion of the brain that is associated with a sense of well-being. It takes only moments to reach that section, then it sits there until it is activated."

"And how is it activated?"

"A wide-range electromagnet pulse activates the compound, causing it to essentially turn this part of the brain off, while simultaneously activating the fight-or-flight impulse in the brain. The result is an intense experience of despair coupled with a sense of panic. We've tested this out independently on subjects as well. The effect was an almost instantaneous attempt to kill themselves."

"So, all together, the subject experiences growing excruciating pain, then despair, with subsequent panic and suicidal ideations."

"Yes, my lord."

"It is perfect."

Sanger hesitated, but clearly had a thought running through his head.

"What is it, doctor?" Luther inquired, still a bit vexed with the man.

"It's just that, this seems like a great deal of effort to go through to have it end in people killing themselves. The weapon I had been working on before your request—the Neutron Vaporizing Device—is much quicker and cleaner path to the same end you desire."

Luther smiled surreptitiously. "Oh, my dear doctor. Do you not know that the end does not justify the means?"

Sanger stared at him blankly.

"Nonetheless, when will this 'less-clean' weapon be ready for us?"

Sanger thought for a minute. "How large a group will we be using this on?"

The Prophet himself pondered this thought, then responded, "It could be as many as two hundred thousand in the initial usage, yet possibly in twelve separate groups, as I have foreseen."

"Parts of the compound need to germinate in the lab for some time. I could have enough ready, I would say, in less than nine months. Though I do have a question about this entire thing."

"Yes?"

"With such an important weapon that could have a monumental impact on the cause, why has the Mystic King himself not been a part of our deliberations?"

iv

The woman continued her flight, with the blue-eyed man on the white horse in pursuit. She ran through a thick wood, seeing the clearing only meters ahead. Once out, she would then be only a short distance from the foot of the dark mountain.

Then I will be safe. I know he cannot follow me there.

She felt a surge of energy as she emerged from the woods, but then she encountered something unexpected.

Stretched out before her the barely distinguishable path came to a fork. To the left, it clearly led to the dark mountain, now looming so close in front of her she would reach it in no time. Yet a different path led to the right, away from the mountain and up to a grassy knoll off in the distance. Though it was quite a way away, the woman could discern a large tree upon the knoll, and it appeared that a figure was sitting at its base.

What could this be?

A light mystical sound pierced the silence, which the woman recognized as music, realizing that it had a certain familiarity about it—from somewhere in the deep recesses of her past. She looked back toward the mountain, certain that safety was fully within her reach, and noting the welcome silence that surrounded it. The sound of galloping suddenly interrupted the scene.

I have to move!

She was about to step onto the path that forked left, but she could not stop herself from again glancing back at the tree on the grassy knoll. The delicate music resumed. She knew this path—just *knew*—that taking it would mean losing nearly all that she held dear to her. But she still somehow could not take her eyes from it.

Why am I hesitating?

7

The Signs of the Times
<<n 3.001>>

VIENNA — An independent study has confirmed what had recently only been conjecture: Mystic Realism is now the most widespread belief system/philosophy in the world.

The study found that the followers of The Way of Mystic Realism now numbered 37% of the global population. When compared against the religions of the world, Christianity places second with 26%, followed by Islam at 18%, and those who claim to hold no particular belief system or worldview at 15%.

The Way of Mystic Realism has spread most rapidly within the Chinese Empire and India, with over 70% of their collective populations claiming allegiance to The Way. In the worldwide population, Buddhism has dwindled to a mere 4% and Hinduism to less than 3%.

Judaism continues to resist the movement, holding at a world population of approximately 20 million, yet still comprising less than 1% of the overall population.

DOMINION

i

Nathaniel sat in the terminal, half in the world and half out, waiting to board a plane destined for Israel. Normally, it would have been impossible for him to be in such a public place without being completely mobbed by adoring fans. But today he was promised *protection*... and this sort of protection provided an anonymity that put the government's Witness Protection Program to shame.

So, he was here today with nothing more than an old acoustic guitar strapped to his back, because his closest friend in the entire world—the man to whom he owed his life—had asked a small favor of him. Who was he to decline?

"You have grown weak, my friend," the Mystic King had said.

Nathaniel sat in his seat, maintaining his zombie-like disposition as the Mystic King circled him.

"You know it is you on whom my favor rests..."

He had given up the interior struggle, and he had found the release to be so... liberating.

"You will go to Israel as a Missionary for The Way. There you will be met by a Rabbi known as Solomon Abrams. He will further your training and formation. With him is an old friend. Together, you will provide a great service to The Way."

"A great service to The Way..." Nathaniel had mumbled.

"As well, two men reside in this nation who will attempt to hunt you down. They desire to sift you like wheat. They go by the names Eli and Hanoch, though in their cunning natures, have used many others. They are confused, but when the appointed time comes, you will be called upon to help them—to help them understand."

"I will help them..." Nathaniel had responded. His eyes momentarily focused on the puncture wounds that still marred the Seal on the back of his right hand.

Jimi T. looked at him somewhat skeptically. He pondered a thought for a moment before speaking.

"I realize this has been extremely difficult for you, Nathaniel, for you existed in the enemy's grasp for sometime. But you are my rock. It is I that gave you life, though you had

been misled to do otherwise. It is he *that wishes you dead, for he knows that you are coming upon the truth."*

"I know the truth…"

"Yes," Jimi T. acknowledged, obviously pleased. *"You do know. But I must tell you, my friend. I can tolerate a doubting Thomas, so long as he does not become my Judas…"*

The boarding announcement was made, and Nathaniel was about to stand when…

His feet would not move.

He tried again, but they still remained glued to the floor. He looked up, preparing to ask for assistance, when he realized every person in the terminal had frozen in place. From somewhere out in the far distance, however, he could hear the sound of music. It was a symphony, to be sure, but in its simplicity—or was it its *complexity*— it struck his ears like no other sound he had ever heard before.

"Nathan…"

A voice called out. A familiar voice. A gentle voice.

He turned his head and saw some movement within the frozen crowd about thirty meters away. He could not make out what it was, only detect its progress, realizing it was moving towards him.

"Nathan, I have come for you."

The stirring came closer, and Nathan was now able to recognize a figure moving towards him. Yet he was not moving around the many airline patrons frozen in place—he was moving *through* them.

The figure finally came to within a recognizable distance, and Nathan set eyes upon his tormentor, Jesse. The well-seasoned anger within Nathan provided him with the energy to stand before this specter from his past.

Jesse smiled. *"You look like hell."*

Nathan was briefly dumbfounded, caught off-guard by the unanticipated lighthearted comment. Yet quickly recovering his sense of bitter anguish, he narrowed his eyes.

"Stay away from me…" he breathed.

Jesse appeared unfazed. *"You still dwell in the valley of darkness, my friend.*

DOMINION

When one is in the fires of Gehenna, everything begins to smell like refuse."

"Please!" Nathan attempted desperately to cling to his forced feelings of antagonism, which clearly desired to dissipate so as to reveal his true sentiments of desperation. He pressed his hands against his temples. *"Please do not abuse me anymore! I can't take it! You are not my friend! You want me to suffer more!"*

But Jesse, now standing only a meter in front of his former band-mate, gently reached out and touched Nathan's shoulder.

"You know this is not true. You have been in the lion's den, as it had to be..."

"Why?" Nathan cried out, looking up with hot tears. *"Why did it have to be that way? Is it fun to jerk me around like a pawn for your own entertainment?"* The tears began to fall from his eyes as he allowed his anger to once again assume dominion. *"It's between you and him; I want no part of it! And I hate you both for it!"*

With that, Nathan collapsed to his knees, sobbing uncontrollably.

Jesse looked down upon his old friend and felt pity for him. *"Your journey is not yet done, and you will face the test one more time. But for now, you must return to our homeland. It is there that you must delve through the ashes and be reborn once again."*

Nathan looked up at him in a puzzled fashion. *"What?"*

But the vision was already fading until...

"Sir?"

Nathan jolted as the image changed. He realized he was standing at the stairs leading to a small jet plane.

"Your hand, sir?"

Nathan looked down and around him, still trying to get his bearings. The lady finally reached over and pulled his hand onto the reader. A bell tone affirmed a proper reading as the woman looked at her screen.

Nathan looked at her curiously. "Where is this plane going?"

The woman smiled in a friendly, yet somewhat concerned fashion. "Well, sir, this plane goes to Wilmington, North Carolina. And according to your e-ticket, you'll be catching an autobus from there to a town called Pergamum."

ASCENSION

ii

"Very well, Mr. Expo, you may address this Council as to your proposal. As you have noted, neither the Charter nor the bylaws expressly forbid one in your position from doing so." Sir Thomas Leese maintained his most stately diplomatic tone. "However, I must state that I strongly oppose your intensive level of involvement and attempted influence with this Council. Despite the fact that you are titled 'Special Envoy' to the Council, you do not represent any nation. In fact, you cannot claim to represent any man's interest except that of your own."

The eyes of all the members of the Global Communion Leadership Council immediately switched, not unlike a tennis match, to the Mystic King, who sat tranquilly at the opposite end of the table. All were aware that the recent cessation of military operations in the major world conflicts had been due mostly to the backdoor negotiations of this enigmatic musician turned diplomatic negotiator. Yet in recent weeks, the inevitable aggressive gestures between the nine major powers of the Earth had re-emerged.

"With all due respect, Sovereign, I do represent over three billion souls upon this planet, who do not delineate their loyalties along national or political lines."

A pregnant pause fell across the room. Eli, sitting at the sovereign's right, looked to Sir Thomas for a response. But Leese, as was characteristic, waited this one out. It was again Jimi T. who broke the silence.

"Council Members, if I may, I would like to introduce you to something I refer to as simply *Peace Proposal*. Some of my assistants will be handing you the proposal for each of your perusals, while I briefly highlight what has been written."

At that moment, several young men stepped forward and began passing out a relatively modest-sized document. Sir Thomas and Eli exchanged uncomfortable glances as Jimi T. Expo continued.

"We are essentially dealing with a very dangerous imbalance of power, in several different arenas. One nation is strong economically, while being weak politically. Another is strong technologically, while weak in social development. However, our greatest threat to world peace is in the imbalance in offensive arms power. As I am sure you all, the leaders of the nine nations and national unions, are aware, despite the fact that internal conditions have improved for each respective nation-state, the possibility of a nuclear war has never been more imminent. Each nation-state can destroy the Earth at least ten times over, and now nuclear weapons could possibly even be carried by citizens… perhaps even disgruntled citizens…

"This proposal will eliminate all of this. All nuclear armaments in each nation or national union, under the supervision of a multinational militia recruited and directed by this Council, will be registered and accounted for. Then, utilizing a formula based on population and landmass, the majority of these weapons of mass destruction will be systematically disarmed and destroyed, so that no one nation or national union can do irreversible damage to the greater part of the Earth."

Jimi T. looked up briefly, noting the intense attentiveness of the Council members upon each word he spoke. The relationship between a number of the members was far from amiable, yet each knew—even grudgingly so—that their nation needed the Global Communion to survive in the new world. Isolation at this juncture would mean sure death at the hands of a multi-headed beast, looking to affirm its claim of dominion. Indeed, collaboration at such high levels was a good thing—so long as you were a part of it.

"In the end, the smallest member-nation, that of Kurdistan, will have the firepower to decimate 50% of the largest nation, currently the Chinese Empire. In turn, the Chinese Empire will have enough firepower to destroy 50% of the nation-states, which would, of course, leave them open to retaliation by the remaining 50%. It is a plan of checks and balances which will both win the world's loyalty and faith in the G.C., while at the same time ensuring that the complete annihilation of the Earth at the hands of a few misguided souls will be an absolute impossibility."

The Council was intrigued, perhaps even convinced at this point… with a few notable exceptions.

"With all due respect," Eli broke in. "Israel is not a member state, and cannot be bound by any resolutions this body moves on."

The Mystic King nodded in acknowledgement. "I do understand this, Ambassador Lige. Yet, being surrounded by forces currently hostile to Israel, I feel your nation is perhaps one that mostly benefits from this proposal, as would be the case with the other non-member states, Honduras and The Vatican."

Before Eli was even able to respond, another member chimed in.

"I move that we fully ratify the Mystic King's proposal as presented," Marta Santeo, the President of the South American Union stated.

Both Eli and Sir Thomas looked to her incredulously.

"But you have not even read the details of the document!" Sir Thomas stated.

"I second the motion!" Sirhan Mahatma, Prime Minister of India followed.

Leese turned his head quickly and then realized that several other Council members were nodding. He looked to Eli, who began to speak.

"Perhaps it would be best to motion for a brief re—"

"With all due respect, sir," Jimi T. cut in. "A motion has already been put on the table and then seconded. I feel it essential that, especially at the tender age and state of this Council, we adhere fully to the doctrines as they have been laid out in the Charter and bylaws, with no deviation."

Sir Thomas Leese fought an instinct to rub his temples in utter frustration, instead folding them in a contemplative fashion. He then looked directly at the Mystic King, paused only a calculated moment, then responded.

"As Sovereign of the Global Communion, it is within my power to postpone a vote on a potentially divisive issue for up to three of the quarterly sessions."

He looked to the remaining members of the Council, to Eli, and then back to Jimi T. himself.

"And at this time, it is my intention to do so."

iii

She blinked her eyes, emerging from the depths of her dream state. Turning instinctively to her right, she saw three figures kneeling at her side. Even before her eyes came fully into focus, she was certain that these blurred apparitions were none other than her loving brothers.

"Avila!" Father Liam cried out.

She knew she had been out for quite some time—her dreams upon dreams were too great in number to be from a single night. Avila tried to speak but realized she could only whisper.

"The Gathering…" she breathed, not even sure how the words reached her lips.

The brothers exchanged looks for a brief moment, expressions of both curiosity and understanding passing between them, then Liam again spoke.

"Hey, sis…it's good to have you back amongst the living."

A gentle smile emerged from her face. "The last time… I… I thought you were on your way to Christopher."

Father Tyler looked briefly to Father Liam, then back at Avila. "Much has happened, dear sister. We have been with Christopher, and for some time now. He has sent his shepherds out into all of Europe. Seven days ago, he instructed us to return to your side."

Her eyes acknowledged the statement with gratitude as they moved to Msgr. Craig.

"And you, dear brother?"

He smiled. "Well, when two men in black show up at your door, it's usually best to comply with their request."

Avila chuckled lightly as she turned her gaze upwards, slowly closing her eyes once again.

"I know now what I must do," she breathed. "I know my purpose."

8

In the end times, when the final strands of the Physical Entity disintegrate, no less than two in three *Řeintül* will be prepared for full assimilation into the *Kóles*, and thus enter into immortality.

However, no more than one in three Followers of Abraham will be saved, for many will cling to the structure of Judaism, not comprehending its full purpose as a provisional vessel and not an entity in and of itself. For this reason also, no more than one in five followers of Mohammed will be prepared for full assimilation.

Yet not a single Christian will be drawn into the *Kóles*, save those that abandon the ways and beliefs of the *Dishalák* and allow the essence of the *Kóles to* flow within them. In the end, all those who deny the eternal sovereignty of the *Kóles*, be they Christian, Jew, or otherwise, will be known as the *Cørtät*.[1]

Sammaet S: 1-6
Book of Given Truths

---

[1] Translation approximation; "Those who deny" or "Those who cut off"

i

Brothers Eli and Hanoch, Phineas, and Father Daniel stood with eager anticipation at the entrance to the Church of Our Lady of Zion. Each had entered the African Union province of Ethiopia separately and inconspicuously so as not to draw attention to this monumental occasion. Eli had been the last to arrive, having flown in from a very unsettling meeting of the newly established Global Communion Leadership Council.

They celebrated a Mass commemorating the Feast of Our Lady of Mount Carmel at daybreak, only a few hours earlier, in central Aksum.

"It is beautiful..." Hanoch marveled. All were fully aware of the magnitude of the event they were about to partake in. Phineas looked over towards the smaller building off to the side of the church. Despite the early hour, many tourists already surrounded it.

"*Mais*, Father. Is that not the structure we are looking for?"

Hanoch shook his head. "No, my son. That is meant to be a diversion. Truly, what we stand before itself is not our desired destination either. That place is much... *deeper.*"

At that moment, the front doors to the church opened, and a contingent of a dozen men stepped forward, separated, and then lined each side of the entrance.

Father Daniel leaned toward Phineas, whispering, "These are the *Falasha Mura.*"

Phineas nodded in acknowledgement as Hanoch and Eli stepped forward, ascending the steps. Father Daniel and Phineas followed behind.

Upon entering the church, the doorway closed behind them. Phineas looked around, marveling at the beauty which his eyes beheld.

Without waiting for further escort, Hanoch moved ahead, ambling towards an altar that sat at the far end of the magnificent structure. The others followed at a distance. Hanoch reached the altar and took a deep, anticipatory breath as he knelt before it. As the others looked on, Hanoch bowed his head, reached his hands forward, and touching the altar, began to pray.

Phineas jolted as Hanoch's hands came in contact with the altar. A sensation he could not adequately describe shot through his entire body. Father Daniel looked to him with concern in his eyes.

"Phinny? Are you all right?"

Phineas looked back to his mentor, the initial wave of fear beginning to dissipate. He smiled as his emerald green eyes began to tear up. Eli also looked at the boy with an expression of curiosity, though it slowly transformed into one of understanding.

"Go," he commanded.

ASCENSION

Phineas looked to him briefly, nodded, then moved towards Hanoch. He stood behind the holy man momentarily before stepping towards the left side of the altar. He glanced briefly at Hanoch, whose lips moved silently in deep prayer. Phineas took a deep breath himself, closed his eyes, then placed his right hand on the altar.

A low rumbling sound suddenly emerged from the immediate area. Hanoch's eyelids opened without delay, his gaze moving to Phineas. The boy looked back, full of awe and wonderment, then he stepped away.

Hanoch, still kneeling, felt the altar begin to tremble and quickly moved back. As the four looked on, the altar lowered into the floor on which they stood. When the top of the altar reached floor level, seven divisions became apparent. The right most division stopped two decimeters below floor level, the next division, two decimeters lower, and so on until all seven sections had formed a stairway leading to a corridor beneath the church.

Eli and Father Daniel stepped forward and looked down the stairway. A flickering light from below suggested that the corridor was lit by torches. Hanoch looked up towards the others, unable to conceal his excitement.

"May the Lord God be with us," he chanted as he rose and moved swiftly down the steps. The others quickly followed.

The corridor below turned and twisted into multiple paths akin to a network of catacombs. The walls were painted with scenes that appeared to be from ancient Egypt and Israel and were full of both hieroglyphics and Hebrew writing. Phineas looked at Hanoch, who after almost an hour of searching was showing some early signs of frustration.

"We have been moving in circles," Eli finally stated, pointing to a picture on the wall. "We have passed this same image of the Queen of Sheba three times, and that of Solomon twice."

"What do you suggest we do?" questioned Hanoch, wiping the sweat from his forehead.

Father Daniel looked to Phineas. "Anything?"

Phineas closed his eyes momentarily. The others watched anxiously as his faced cocked briefly in a curious fashion, then went blank again. Finally, he opened his eyes, shaking his head.

"*Mo chagren*, Father. I can't get anything, I…"

Hanoch stepped forward and interrupted. "No... you felt something. We were all witness to it upon your face. What was it, my son?"

Phineas began shaking his head. "No... I... I thought I was sensing something, but then I—"

"Please, Phinny," urged Father Daniel, anxious himself for any divine inspiration.

"I thought I heard... I thought I heard *music*?"

"Music?" Eli exclaimed with a clear sense of intrigue.

Instinctively, they all fell silent. From somewhere in the deepest depths of the catacombs, they detected a sound... the distinct voice of a young boy singing.

Hanoch looked at Eli with visible animation. He started humming lightly to himself, then a moment later began to quietly sing along. "It is... it is the song of our people, it is ancient Hebrew... *I will sing to the Lord, for he is gloriously triumphant; horse and chariot he has cast into the sea.*"

He turned towards the sound, and the foursome moved swiftly through the tunnels with renewed energy, following the melodic voice which beckoned to them. Minutes later, they emerged into an immense, circular room. Though they could look upwards and see the ceiling a good twenty meters above, they had before them a wall, perhaps three meters high, running in both directions and forming an inner circle within the room.

"The seven concentric circles!" Eli asserted as the young boy's voice continued to sound out.

The four skirted along the outside of the wall until they found a break, from which they would descend by steps another three meters into a smaller inner ring. Fueled by the excitement and the hauntingly mesmerizing voice of the child, the foursome navigated their way through the initial six rings, and then came upon...

A small dark-skinned boy, perhaps no more than ten years of age. He ceased to sing upon seeing the four men before him. After a momentary expression of surprise, a gentle smile came forth from his face.

"You have come," he spoke in Hebrew, gazing directly at Hanoch and Eli.

Hanoch could not keep the tears from falling as he gazed at the Ark resting behind the young boy.

ASCENSION

"Yes," the boy spoke, as if reading Hanoch's thoughts. "It has been my honor to serve as Sentinel of the Ark for the past three years. My family has guarded the Covenant with our lives for forty generations. I am the last. I am Menelik the Second, and I am at your disposal."

The boy stood aside, making a path from Hanoch and Eli to the Ark of the Covenant, which held fragments of the bread called 'manna', the priestly rod of Moses' brother, Aaron, and the remains of the tablets—the Ten Commandments—written directly by the hand of a God who seemed strangely quiet in the present age. Hanoch moved forward, reached out, and began caressing the Ark.

"So then," Eli addressed the boy, having been taken aback at the mention of the boy's name. "You are a direct descendant of Menelik, son of Solomon?"

"I am," the boy responded. "The single and the final descendant of the House of Solomon."

Eli nodded curiously as he joined his comrade at the foot of the Ark.

At that moment, Menelik and Phineas' eyes met. In a fleeting instant, only witnessed by Father Daniel, Menelik's eyes rolled back into his head, and he staggered a step backwards. The priest looked to Phineas, who glanced back at him with an expression of confusion and angst. Menelik's eyes opened, and he looked warily towards Phineas.

"You bear the mark of the Elect."

"I do," Phineas replied guardedly.

"How can this be?"

Phineas looked to Father Daniel for clarification, but received none. "*Mo pa konmprann*, Father," he breathed, clearly agitated and confused.

Menelik himself looked at Father Daniel incredulously, then back to Phineas. "Your time has been shortened." Then turning back to Father Daniel he added, "Can you not see?"

Before the moment could go any further, Eli and Hanoch returned, standing at either side of the boy Menelik. To the awe of Phineas and Father Daniel, both seemed to have peculiarly increased in stature. Menelik dropped to his knees as at least two-dozen men entered the room, performing the same act of homage.

"The Coptic Priests," Father Daniel whispered as he and Phineas knelt.

DOMINION

From somewhere in the depths of the catacombs, a gong-like sound rang out. In a voice filled with authority, Hanoch spoke.

"On this day, Menelik, descendant of Solomon and the Queen of Sheba, I relieve you of your charge as Sentinel. You and your ancestors have served well."

As if on cue, Eli then spoke. "The day is upon us for the rebuilding of the Temple, where the Ark of the Covenant will be placed once again, never to be removed. Prepare ye for the Kingdom of God!"

The contingent cried out in unison in some unknown tongue, and Menelik rose. Eli leaned towards the boy and whispered, "Do come with us, Menelik, share in the glory which you have made possible."

But the young boy shook his head. "I am grateful, but I cannot, for my time is not of this age, but of the next."

With that, Menelik grasped both Eli and Hanoch's hands and spoke out.

"The Witnesses of the Latter Days have come to rightfully lay claim to the Covenant of the almighty *Adonai*. Behold! That all may see... unto their people hath returned... Enoch and Elijah!"

ii

Nathan stepped off of the jet way and quickly spotted a bathroom across the way. He briefly glanced up at the monitor above him and noted the date:

Neöret 3.030

That can't be right, he mused. *That flight wasn't even two hours... let alone four weeks.*

He dismissed it as a malfunction with the monitor and continued towards the bathroom. He suddenly felt a dreamy sensation begin to overcome him.

No... not now... I have to keep my wits about me.

Nathan quickened his pace, entered the bathroom (he had never been able to get used to the multi-gender nature of these things these days) and moved quickly to the sink, throwing water on his face in the hope that it would make the sensation go away. For the moment, it seemed to do the trick as he turned and moved towards the first available stall he could find. He opened the door, stepped in, and…

…he was standing at the edge of a clearing, a sparse wooded area to his back. He quickly shot his gaze in all directions.

I've been here before.

Nathan looked up ahead and upon a grassy knoll he saw the tree he had discovered in a previous vision. At that time, a young boy had been at its base, but this time the boy was nowhere to be seen.

He moved towards the tree, which had clearly grown several feet since he had last been here. He listened for the wind-chime-like music that had accompanied his previous vision, but all he could hear was the sound of the gentle breeze. Curiously, however, amidst the light gusts, Nathan felt he could hear a number of whispering voices, though he could not quite make out any specific words.

He arrived by the tree and looked down upon the gravestones he had seen before. He gathered he was at the resting place of his old friend Jonathan—here called by his apparent real name, Jesse—along with the rest of his family. Nathan shuddered slightly when he saw the headstone for Alexandre Nesterov.

I'm glad you're dead, old man.

Suddenly, something passed not more than a few centimeters in front of Nathan's face, and he cried out as he stumbled backwards.

He looked to his left to see the back of a figure approaching the tree. The man acted as if he was distraught, and at least at the moment, he did not seem to even notice that Nathan was present. The man turned, and Nathan gasped…

Oh my G—

The figure looked in his direction, but still did not seem to see him.

"Who is that? Is someone there?"

Nathan stood frozen as he looked upon the paramedic with the crown of thorns tattoo on his neck. He was much paler, almost sickly, and seemed to have a completely different spirit about him. The man who at one time exuded confidence and peace was now quivering and nervous.

"Can't you see me?" Nathan inquired.

The man looked all about him, but did not seem to see Nathan until he stepped towards him. He was suddenly startled and stepped back. Nathan watched in curiosity as the man's body seemed to flicker—even momentarily draw apart—before pulling back together.

"Who are you?" the paramedic inquired, with a voice that seemed to resonate with a rapidly dissipating echo.

"Why... I'm Nathan... Nathan Freeman. You helped me. You've been to my home."

The expression on the man's face was one of utter confusion. *"I do not know you."* He appeared to ponder a thought for a moment more. *"But you say... you say you know me. Who... who am I?"*

Nathan was puzzled as to what was actually happening, and he could not hide his sense of disappointment. A part of him, it seemed, had always hoped that another encounter with this man would take place. A part of him craved that peace which no one else Nathan knew seemed to possess. And now it was apparently gone.

"You... you are a paramedic. You help people. You told me your name was Ralph."

"Ralph?"

"Yes... Ralph. You are a paramedic in Los Angeles."

The figure thought for a moment, and then his body once again began to... *separate.* His expression as his molecules seemed to draw back together suggested this experience was not without discomfort.

"I do not know of what you speak. It seems... it seems I am lost."

He looked up to the tree and reached his hand towards it. What seemed like a localized flash manifested itself, and the eyes of the man once called Ralph momentarily rolled back into his head. It was clear that whatever was happening to him was painful.

"I keep coming back to this tree... it is the only thing that seems familiar to me, so I will wait here."

"I wouldn't sweat it much," Nathan responded, seemingly not too concerned. *"Really, this is just another hallucination I'm having. You have clearly represented a source of hope in my mind—but now it seems my mind wishes to make you impotent and unable to help me. Seems that even in my hallucinations I can't catch a break."*

ASCENSION

The Ralph-like figure looked disheartened. *"Then I am not real?"*

Nathan shook his head. *"No... I'm afraid you are not... at least not here. It seems I'm slowly going mad, but I'll tell you what. I'll get back to L.A. and find the real you... then maybe we can go out for a beer or something. Cool?"*

The lost look did not depart from the man's face. *"You... you said that I help people?"*

Nathan nodded solemnly. *"Yeah, that you do. You're like a regular guardian angel... though perhaps in my mind I've made you out to be more than you are."*

The man's body seemingly winked in and out of existence one more time as he grasped a hold of the tree trunk.

"I am a guardian..." the man whispered to himself, more trying to convince himself than to truly seek the response of another. Nathan stood without responding, still a bit perplexed as to how he had been drawn into this scene.

"Please," the Ralph-like man then pleaded. *"If I am not real, and this is all in your mind, then when you depart from this place, I will be no more. Please... go... I beg you. I cannot tell you the suffering my presence here causes me..."*

iii

King Adar Cyrul stood before the mirror trying to discern whether he even recognized himself anymore. It had only been a few hours since his nephew, Father Daniel, and the boy Phineas had departed. To say that it had been an uncomfortable meeting was an understatement.

"I am curious, Uncle," Father Daniel had said. "The last time we spoke, your nation was struggling economically... severely, as I remember. Now, in just a few short years, I see affluence all around this place. Even the superliner cruise ships Kurdistan provided for transferring Christians out of the North American Union. Where did all this wealth come from?"

Cyrul had found himself immediately defensive. "What are you suggesting, Daniel? I am the leader of a nation—small, but proud. Yet without benefactors, my country would not only be crushed by the surrounding Islamic nations, my people would starve!"

"Benefactors?" Father Daniel had suddenly looked concerned. "Uncle, what have you done?"

"I have done nothing that any leader of a people would not do! There are those out there who believe that a small country such as ours has every right to not only exist, but also thrive! If these benefactors decide to be generous on our behalf, who am I to deny their generosity?"

"Their generosity? And in exchange for what, Uncle?"

"You," Cyrul breathed angrily, taking a tone he had never used with his nephew before, "have the luxury of focusing only on the spiritual. I must make decisions in the temporal, in the interest of my people. Your judgment has no place here, Daniel!"

The discussion had ended in that manner, and Father Daniel had pushed no further. Yet one phrase from their confrontation continued to return to the king's thoughts.

...in exchange for what, Uncle?

It really had not seemed like too much to ask in return for hundreds of billions of dollars pumped into his desperate economy. And Col. Bildeberger had even thrown in the twenty-four superliner cruise ships, *gratis*, for use in developing a thriving vacation cruise business which would further provide income, create jobs, and cultivate a much-needed global feeling of goodwill—if not sympathy—for the tiny Christian nation. Certainly, the superliners had initially seemed like an odd offer to a landlocked nation like Kurdistan, but Bildeberger had even facilitated the handover of the small Kuwaiti Island of Failaka to Kurdish sovereignty, not only for a port in the Persian Gulf, but to be developed into a much-desired international resort island. It was beyond anything that Cyrul could have possibly dreamed of.

...in exchange for what, Uncle?

It had seemed like so little. Bildeberger only requested that the king make the superliners available to the North American Union for the transfer of the millions of Christians out of their union and to the nation of Honduras. At the last minute, Bildeberger had contacted Cyrul and informed him that he would supply the crews for each ship, though he asked the king to "keep this under his hat," as he wanted Kurdistan to receive full international credit for the act of generosity. Cyrul had experienced a brief moment of apprehension, but not wishing to go against the greatest benefactor in the history of his country, he had obliged.

ASCENSION

The superliners had now been returned. Yet what Cyrul did keep from his nephew was the report he received, admittedly unsubstantiated, yet from what he had considered a reliable source in the past. The superliners made over a thousand trips between them over the six-week period, but only seventeen were actually confirmed to have reached the isolated nation of Honduras.

...in exchange for what, Uncle?

Cyrul looked with horror upon his reflection, not fully recognizing the man that looked back at him.

"What have I done?"

9

i

Phineas and Father Daniel sat quietly in their seats thirty-five thousand feet above the Atlantic Ocean. It had been both a wonderful and grueling three weeks gallivanting throughout the Holy Land of old. A final stop in Medugorje had proved to be quite invigorating. This last part, re-entry into the North American Union, was a bit anxiety-provoking, as Father Daniel's priestly status now designated him a fugitive in the region. A falsified passport, along with an undercover member of the Christian Resistance serving in customs, would be their cover. The rest was up to God.

Phineas looked over to his mentor, who rested peacefully with his eyes closed. Though the entire trip could be described as nothing other than providential and blessed, there was one little piece that vexed Phineas.

"Your time has been shortened…"

The phrase, spoken by the boy called Menelik, hearkened back to another that had been stated a short time before.

"…take solace, young man, in that I will cut your days short…"

He pondered the meaning that could be attributed to these very similar phrases. Clearly, there was a common thread. Father Daniel had not seemed to pay much mind to the comment provided by Menelik… but then again, he was unaware of the prophecy offered by the Mystic King in Phineas' vision.

"Excuse me, sir."

A voice pulled Phineas out of his reverie. A hand bearing the Seal of Mystic Realism came across the pullout tray in front of him.

Phineas jumped, startling both himself and the flight attendant who was reaching for his empty glass.

She immediately attempted to apologize. "Oh, I'm sorry, sir; I did not mean to…"

And then her voice trailed off, and Phineas looked up to her, becoming conscious of the fact that she was now staring at his forehead. He quickly reached up, realizing at that moment that his bandana had slipped, and his mark of the Christian Elect was partly revealed. He hastily attempted to cover it, but it was too late. A look of both anger and disgust came across the flight attendant's face.

"Your kind make me sick," she breathed barely above a whisper through clenched teeth. "You'll ruin it for all of us!"

Phineas dropped his gaze, not wishing to foster a scene. But as he looked up, the attendant might as well have screamed at the top of her lungs. All eyes on the plane were now upon him. A woman in the next row pulled her child away, shielding his eyes.

Phineas blinked, as he now seemed to see a red… *glow*… emanating from the eyes of these people. A cold sweat began to break out across his entire body as the passengers stood, their faces contorting, reshaping into something that could only be described as… *reptilian*.

Now standing, these horrific distortions began to move towards him as long and thin tongues extended and retracted from their hissing mouths. Fangs emerged as they called out in unison:

"CØRTÄT!"

"Phinny!"

A voice accompanied by a physical jolt shook him. Phineas looked up to see that everyone was calmly sitting in their seats, going about their own business. He looked to his right to see a perplexed look on the face of Father Daniel.

A familiar voice called out across the intercom.

"Good morning, ladies and gentlemen, we've landed at Rochester International Airport. We hope the flight was both comfortable and enlightening to you all."

Phineas looked up and met eyes with the flight attendant from his vision, who smiled slyly back at him, intercom in hand.

"My name is Jenny Carlin, and on behalf of the captain, crew, and the entire One Globe Alliance, I wish you all have a good day, and may the Spirit be with you."

ii

Sir Thomas Leese sat in his study, staring at the picture situated on the far right-hand corner of his desk. The photo had been taken only a few months earlier and depicted him and his nephew, Adam, smiling and waving during their ski trip to the Swiss Alps.

Tears began to well up in his eyes as he thought back to the first time he had laid eyes on the boy. Adam had only been a few days old when his parents were mercilessly slain before his non-comprehending eyes by several remnants of the defunct Irish Republican Militia.

And today, Sir Thomas would endure further suffering for the good deeds of his past. He found himself falling into a dreamy reverie…

He saw himself sitting in the waiting room of the hospital, approaching his tenth month of marriage to the love of his life, anxiously waiting for the doctor to emerge and to tell him that, despite the complications which had taken place, he was to be a proud papa. Instead, the surgeon's grim face revealed what he would not require words to tell… that Thomas was now alone in a way he could have never imagined… a childless widower.

The scene transformed, and Sir Thomas saw himself sitting at a table, signing into law the United Ireland Charter, only weeks after his election as Prime Minister of the United Kingdom. He was actually being hailed as the "second coming of Saint Patrick" after passing this piece of legislation. The peace agreement ended generations of bloodshed in the region, created a single, sovereign Ireland, but it also placed a few militant radicals in the I.R.M. out of work. Though Sir Thomas knew that some of these people would seek revenge on him, he had not thought that the target could have been someone other than himself...

He then saw himself, standing across the busy Ipswich street from his sister and brother-in-law, waiting to enter St. Aidan's pub for lunch in preparation for the infant Adam's baptism. Thomas' sister put his nephew down just for a moment to write their names on the waiting list outside, when Sir Thomas saw the car... then his sister's body convulse... before actually hearing the shots. This was quickly followed by the same movement by his brother-in-law. The vision faded with a hysterically crying child in the carriage, covered in the blood of his parents.

The final transition had Sir Thomas bringing young Adam Moore home for the first time... guilt-ridden beyond comprehension, yet resolved to raise the boy as his own.

His eyes came back into focus on the clock in his private study—one of twelve private studies that were his to utilize—this time at G.C. Six on a remote island off of the coast of Africa. The clock read three p.m. on the dot. Though Thomas was still experiencing the dreamy state, the images had dissipated, and he sat reflecting on his years of raising Adam. He could honestly say that despite the multitude of accolades for his public service, he found the rearing of this young lad to be the most rewarding experience of his life. Adam was now a fine young man of fifteen, and through Sir Thomas' gentle counsel, had come to start the process of questioning—on his own capabilities of reason—some of the actions and thoughts of his one-time idol, Jimi T. Expo. Adam had even taken the name of St. Thomas for his Confirmation a month earlier. Yes, this young boy was sure to have a significant impact on the future of this perilous world... one day, it would be his time to shine.

And with this in mind, Sir Thomas had resolved what he must do...

He provided a sad, somewhat nostalgic smile. It was not long ago that he was seemingly untouchable. He had thought his work in public service had come to an end when he stepped down as Chairman of the U.L.D.N. His passion for humanity, unequivocal fairness, and gentle wielding of authority had propelled him to a status near Sainthood, a position which his humble nature had difficulty accepting.

If only I had stopped there, he thought sadly to himself.

But he had not. When the Global Communion was established, his services were aggressively besought, as no other name was even mentioned in reference to the position of sovereign. Even the Most Holy Father, Peter II, had petitioned him to embrace this vocation. Sir Thomas, with some final coaxing, had humbly accepted the position, recognizing the inherent dangers of the office and the flaws in the general concept, yet he was admittedly intrigued by the opportunity to be a part of bringing about an authentic world peace.

And in all good conscience, Sir Thomas immediately set about his task of confronting what he now recognized as the greatest threat to that peace:

The Way of Mystic Realism.

Though Jimi T. Expo, the alleged 'Mystic King' and designer of the G.C., had seemingly accepted Sir Thomas' position on the matter as merely a ideological difference of opinion, it would soon be evident that these differences would not be left to benign philosophical discussions. And following the move by Sir Thomas to quash the proposal of Jimi T. Expo to the G.C., the gauntlet had been dropped.

It was not two weeks later when the first blemish appeared on Adam's body.

More followed, a few each day, seemingly sapping the very life out of the boy. Bedridden and in excruciating pain, the doctors could not make head nor tail of the mysterious disease, yet they were unequivocal in their prognosis; the boy would be dead within the week.

Abraham… how could you do it? Isaac was just a boy…

Sir Thomas—anguished beyond any ability to think with the unfettered clarity that had been his hallmark in public life—was at a complete loss as what to do.

Until tonight.

While sponging the nearly lifeless boy down only a few hours earlier, Sir Thomas had watched in horror as the blemishes seemingly altered in their coloration, forming an unquestionable pattern, spelling out two words on the boy's abdomen which sent chills down Thomas' spine:

ONE LIFE

Though a third party may have found these words to be no more than a curious riddle, Sir Thomas knew intuitively the directive which was being placed upon him. Those who would view him as the adversary to humanity's progress would require of him only one life; his own or that of his nephew.

So there was really no decision at all, and the brief wrestle with his conscience was quashed by his own sense of impotence confronting the reality of the imminent death of the boy. Now that he had completed the entire prescription of his heart medication, there was also no turning back.

Sir Thomas hummed an old hymn as his eyesight began to fade, and his ears apparently began to play tricks on him. The floorboards from upstairs began to creak, and he could swear that he heard the sounds of footfalls upon the steps.

Just before darkness permanently set in on his world, a blur of a figure descended to the bottom of the stairs.

"Uncle!" it called out of the murkiness. "I am better!"

Darker and darker, Sir Thomas' last intention in this life was to attempt, albeit unsuccessfully, to chastise this taunting demon.

"Uncle?"

iii

On the day of *Neöret* 3.046, Sister Sawlus drove at a comfortable speed through the back roads of New Jersey with the car-top down and functioning fully on manual. She loved these opportunities to disengage the *i-Nav* system—one of the perks given only to the few who held positions of privilege—feeling as free and powerful on the road as she recalled in her teenage years. She looked over at Caleb and smiled as she reached over and caressed his hairless head. It had been fifteen months since his induction into the *Neo Mîstè*, but still this look seemed somewhat of a novelty to her.

Caleb smiled back at her. She admired how handsome he was becoming, especially in his bright red uniform. Even though she was seeing less and less of him—with the Lodge meetings, Mystic ceremonies, and Restoration rallies—Sawlus felt happier than she had ever been. And now with Jimi T. Expo's personal interest in her son, Caleb would be assured a place of prominence within The Way.

This was to be Caleb's first month-long mission, where he would travel to citizens' homes, proclaiming the good news of the *Kôles* and seeking out converts who desired true liberation. Yet despite the fact that she could not have scripted a more perfect life, Sawlus still experienced an unexpected twinge of sadness as she pulled up to the drop-off point.

However, the excitement in Caleb's eyes was immeasurable, so she did not allow him to see the sadness in her own. Several other youths were already there, and some others were saying their good-byes to their parents.

"Well, looks like it's time, kiddo. Last chance to change your mind."

Caleb looked excitedly at his mother. "Not for all the *Cortät* on a stick! I've been waiting so long for this!"

Sawlus smiled and opened her arms. "Give Mommy a hug."

Caleb did as he was told, then got out of the car and headed for the others. Sawlus spotted Tæsír Hoc, fresh back from his trip to Palestine, who waved to her and winked. She produced a deliberately fake smile and pulled away before he got any ideas about coming over to speak with her.

The drive home to Florham Park seemed to take much longer than her drive up. In fact, Sawlus was sure that she had made a wrong turn—one clear *disadvantage* of disengaging the *i-Nav* system—as she no longer recognized the road she was on. Yet still feeling the euphoria only slightly tainted by maternal sadness, she decided against switching the system back on. As was her habit when thinking she was on the wrong trail, Sawlus began driving faster, hoping to quickly spot a familiar landmark which would remind her that she was indeed on the right track.

But this was not the case, and twenty minutes later, Sawlus found herself trying unsuccessfully to simultaneously restart an obviously faulty *i-Nav* system while negotiating the twists in the road which she had never intended to be on in the first place. She finally got the system to acknowledge the route she was on, and was about to look for a sign to the next town, called Askus, when she looked up and…

There, in the middle of the road, perhaps twenty meters in front of her, stood a rogue of a man. She met his eyes only momentarily before she swung the wheel to avoid him. She attempted to correct her vehicle, but the turn was too sharp, and she crashed through the barrier. A split second later she was airborne, careening through the air straight for a patch of trees.

Sawlus did not know what happened from that point onwards. She suddenly became aware of an extremely bright light. Looking up from her landing spot, she saw standing before her the blue-eyed man from her visions. She looked up at him to see that his hands were still bound. He looked upon her with saddened eyes.

"Sister, why do you oppress the Body with such virulence?"

Sawlus looked up at the figure as best she could, but found that she was unable to do so due to the brightness that emanated from him. Still, there was a definite familiarity about this specter... a familiarity she even sensed in her dreams. Yet it was nothing she could put her finger on at the moment.

"Do I know you?" she asked meekly.

"I am called Jesse, though I have gone by many other names. I am the Fruit of Humanity... as the Body suffers, I suffer. It is the Bride of the Redeemer whom you persecute. Will you not relent?"

Sawlus shook her head, trying to overcome the greatest sense of fear she had experienced since her father's death.

"If the Redeemer you speak of is called Jesus," she began, *"then I do not know him. He is a myth. Had he been... had he been the loving deity he was purported to be, he would not have abandoned me when I needed him most."*

A gentle, compassionate smile came across Jesse's face, though the sadness in his eyes remained. *"He has always been with you, Sister, and in my presence He speaks to you now, in your time of greater need."*

Sawlus attempted to respond, trying to rekindle the anger which had sustained her over the past seven years, but she was somehow unable to do so. A moment later, she found herself beginning to sob.

"M-My father... you let my father die... he was a good man! He obeyed your laws, but you let him d-die!" She stopped temporarily, trying to regain some sense of composure, then continued. *"When I was there with him on his deathbed, I did not see the peaceful serenity that you had promised awaited him upon his exit from this world and entrance into your so-called Kingdom. I saw fear... not peace... fear!"*

She was about to continue, feeling her anger slowly seeping back into her spirit, permitting her the strength to stand up to this figure when...

She could speak no longer.

"Your father did many great deeds on this Earth, and through his love of his Redeemer, though he died a death great in suffering, he has been greatly rewarded in our Father's Kingdom."

At this point, Jesse's tone became sterner, yet not reflecting condemnation, but fraternal concern. *"Still, it is not for you to question the works of our Father. You have engaged in many acts of wickedness in these years... acts for which you must make atonement. Therefore, you will cease to speak until you are called by your Christian name from the lips of another, a name which I now return to you."*

Sawlus felt the last bit of anger suddenly drain out of her, abandoning the great void which had formed within her on the day her father died.

"Your father asked that I pass on this gift to you."

And in an instant, Sawlus sensed the presence of her father encompass her as the void became filled with a paternal sense of love and security. The tears spontaneously streamed forth from her eyes.

"Your sins have been washed away by your tears and are forgiven by our Redeemer, but the soul of your son is in great jeopardy. You must seek out the Earthen Pastor in a town known as Pittsford. He will help you fulfill the calling given to you at your conception, and he will assist you in the drawing of your son."

The woman stood from her place, and though she could still not fully discern his face in the brightness, she reached for the ropes binding his hands. But the image began to swirl, and a moment later, she lost consciousness.

10

i

"I cannot believe what I am reading!" a fuming Caliph Ali Bakr of the Arabian Empire bellowed. "You cannot do this! You have no right!"

Jimi T. sat back in his seat at the head of the table, his hands together with forefingers touching his lips in a pensive position.

"But I can, my brother. It is clearly stated in the statutes that the sovereign may enact any decree in a state of emergency with the consent of only one third of the Council, of whose signatures you will see at the bottom of that document you have before you."

The Caliph's hands clenched and he spoke bitterly through his teeth. "And to which emergency are you referring, may I ask?"

Jimi T. lowered his hands, placing them both flatly on the table. "Losing the sovereign of this Council within the first year of its existence is nothing short of a worldwide crisis. The preservation of the Global Communion is paramount to the future of our world's survival."

Eli watched on, utterly perplexed. Before him was a decree granting the Nation of Israel full rights to rebuild the Most Holy Jewish Temple. This was to be part of a seven-year protective order, providing the Jews special status among nations. He reflected briefly on the previous seven-year pact that he and his deceased friend, Ibn Fatimah, had crafted. Long forgotten due to dramatically transforming world events, its consummation was to have taken place only months ago.

Your ways, Elohim… they are… mysterious. Do I unwittingly play into the will of your adversary?

"How does giving the Jewish slime that which rightfully belongs to the Islamic tradition relate to your worldwide crisis?" Bakr challenged loudly.

The Mystic King leaned forward and spoke firmly, yet calmly. "You are very nearsighted, my brother, and appear to be putting the wants of your one nation before the needs of the many. The Jewish faith was instituted by the Spirit of the *Kôles*, and has been vital in drawing back a countless number of souls who would have otherwise been lost. It was the only structure which prevented the entire dissolution of the Spiritual Entity within the *Čidentůl*… and for this great deed, the Jews have been persecuted throughout the ages, by Christians and Muslims alike!"

The entire Council sat, somewhat surprised, yet mesmerized by the conviction in the Mystic King's voice.

"The persecution ends here. Those of the Jewish faith will have seven years to complete their spiritual cycle, over which time, they may bring closure to the greatest religion—and the greatest earthen analogy of the *Kôles*—in the history of mankind."

Bakr's teeth continued to clench, yet no words emerged. Hot tears clung to his eyelids.

"Sovereign," another voice from the table spoke.

ASCENSION

A slight trace of a smile emerged from Jimi T. Expo's face. For some reason, hearing his title spoken from the lips of this particular representative was especially pleasing.

"The Council recognizes Brother Eli."

Eli stared back at the Mystic King, only momentarily fazed by the title which had been bestowed upon him for the moment. "In reference to this decree, entitled *The Jewish Solution*, I too respectfully request to go on record as dissenting from its ratification."

ii

Sawlus slowly pulled her car up to the end of the street. She tried to be discreet, watching her son and another boy parking their solar-bikes and walking up to a house. It had been a difficult task to ascertain Caleb's whereabouts, especially for someone who no longer had the luxury of speech. Yet after ten agonizing days, she was finally able to get the break she needed.

She had spent most of this time fluctuating between a saving peace, feeling as if the weight of the world had been lifted from her, and the depths of despair, reflecting on the deeds she had done over the past seven years. How many souls had she shattered?

Her disappearance would be noticed soon, if it had not been already. Sawlus reflected on her vision as she watched her son and another youth speak to the woman who had just opened the door. What permanent damage had she done to him? How had she gotten so far off track? She pondered for a moment on Caleb's father and a chill swept through her.

Suddenly, the woman at the door became visibly agitated and slammed it shut.

Poor Caleb, Sawlus thought. *She probably hurt his little feelings.*

However, she quickly noted that the expression on Caleb's face was not what one would expect from a boy who had his feelings hurt. He looked over to the other boy and smiled.

Sawlus watched with curiosity as Caleb pulled a small canister from the other boy's backpack. He pointed it at the front door, and a thin stream of fire shot forth from it. Caleb burned the Seal of Mystic Realism into the door, and wrote, as Sawlus watched on in horror, "*Cortät Scum*".

The door continued to burn as the woman opened it and screamed. Caleb and the boy laughed and then ducked away as the woman tried frantically to put out the fire. As they ran, Caleb, looked up and briefly caught his mother's eye. Sawlus attempted to duck, but it was too late.

"What is it?" the other boy asked, still panting with excitement.

Caleb had a confused look on his face. "It is my mother…"

The boy's eyes lit up. "That's Sister Sawlus! Introduce me, man!"

Caleb looked to the boy and shook his head as he moved towards his mother. "Some other time, Abram."

Sawlus felt her heart rate begin to accelerate as her son approached. She had prayed this would be easy. After all, he was *her* son, right? Only, considering what had just transpired, she found herself almost questioning this notion. In an instant, Caleb was at the window of her vehicle.

"What are you doing here, Mother?" he inquired, shaking Sawlus from her brief reverie.

She opened her mouth to speak but quickly recalled that she could not.

"What's wrong?" Caleb further inquired. "Why aren't you speaking?"

Sawlus quickly grabbed a scrap of paper, found a pencil, and scribbled out a note:

I can't explain right now, my love,
but I need you to come with me right away…

Caleb looked curiously at her. "You know I cannot do that, Mother. This is the first leg of my mission. I must complete it… what exactly is going on?"

Sawlus looked back at him in exasperation and felt her anxiety increase as another car pulled around the corner, which the boy called Abram promptly walked to and began speaking with the driver. He nodded a few times, then pointed in their direction. Sawlus quickly scribbled out a second note:

Come with me now, Caleb!

He read it and shook his head once again. "I cannot… what's

happened, Mother?"

Sawlus looked over and saw the vehicle pull away from Abram and begin to approach her. Her eyes widened; she reached out and grabbed Caleb by the arm, attempting to pull him in through the car window.

"Mother!" he screamed as the other car suddenly screeched its tires, accelerating towards them. Sawlus tried to reach around with her other arm to pull Caleb by his belt buckle, but she suddenly felt a stabbing pain in her hand.

She screamed out silently and released her grip as she realized Caleb had bitten her. Blood flowed freely out of the back of her hand, providing a macabre image as it covered her Seal.

Caleb sprinted for the other vehicle, and Sawlus quickly slammed her car into drive, hitting the accelerator at the same time. She spun the tires, and momentarily looked back to catch Caleb's stare.

He looked upon her with the eyes of a stranger.

iii

He had lost time again... he was certain of it.

Nathan pulled the stamped autobus ticket from his pocket, which clearly marked that his trip began on the third year and second day of the *Neöret*. Yet, as he looked up at the bus station's digital calendar, it read "n. 3.057."

That is almost two months... where have I been?

He recalled falling asleep on the autobus as restless dreams pervaded his spirit. The only thing he could recall was a dream of the paramedic named Ralph, of whom he had experienced in a vision just prior. This time, Ralph was engulfed in an endless, dark abyss, bearing an expression of utter disorientation. In the vision Nathan had stood before him, but again, no recognition passed across the face of the man who had once offered a kindness to him.

Now Nathan stood at the bus station, his old acoustic guitar strapped to his back, staring out at the center of the town called Pergamum. As a youth, this was the new home that was to end all his and his family's troubles. Looking back now, he wondered if his parents ever really knew what trouble was.

Are you proud of me, Dad? he thought, half-expecting an answer.

Nathan began to walk, not necessarily in any planned direction, but just because it felt right to do so. The town seemed completely deserted. There were markings of both Mystic Realism as well as Christianity all over the buildings, which appeared to be abandoned, gutted, and some even burned.

His eye was temporarily caught by a phone booth in disrepair. A wave of sadness swept over him as he recalled hearing of his parents death on that very phone. And his thoughts slipped, regretfully, to the call he had made immediately following the news...

Nathan walked for the better part of an hour without seeing anyone. He now realized he was headed in the direction of Jonathan's house.

As he turned the corner onto the street of his old friend, his heart dropped as he saw that the first few houses had been burned to the ground.

What am I doing here? It was just a crazy dream... nothing more.

But then everything stopped. Nathan felt a moment of vertigo when it seemed as if all sound had been sucked from the scene. He looked down the street, now seeing that *every* house had been leveled. Every house, that is, except for Jonathan's.

Jesse's!

There was debris covering every centimeter surrounding the property, along with more graffiti on the sidewalk and pavement by the house. Yet the yard and the house itself were immaculate—as if they had been untouched by time.

The scene grew in its surrealism as Nathan walked up to the front door. He thought he could detect the sound of music from inside. Some of that old classical stuff that...

His mind spun as he reached up and knocked on the door.

The music ceased.

Footsteps.

"Why, Nathan! So good to see you!"

He looked up to see Vannie Storm standing in the doorway, smiling as if the world depended on it, and adorned in a simple yet brilliantly white dress.

Nathan stared at her, his mouth agape.

"Are you all right, Nathan?" she inquired, her expression becoming one

of concerned curiosity.

He struggled to spit out, *"Is Jonathan home?"*

She smiled a somewhat sad smile as she shook her head. *"No I'm sorry, Nathan, Jesse has moved on, and it seems he can't find his way back. I had hoped that perhaps you were him when I heard the knock."*

Nathan looked down to his feet, suddenly feeling ashamed. *"I-I'm sorry, Mrs. Storm. I thought he might have... I... I'm just sorry. I didn't mean to disturb you."*

She smiled gently at him. *"Oh, Nathan, it's no trouble at all. It's been so long... and only he visits me now."*

Nathan looked up curiously. *"Who's 'he'?"*

A troubled look set in on the woman's face, and she looked as if she was holding back tears with all her might. *"My n-nephew..."*

Nathan stood frozen in place as a chill shot down his spine. *"I should go..."*

The woman he knew as Mrs. Storm raised a hand to her mouth, restraining a cry, and nodded slowly. *"That would probably be best."*

Nathan hesitated and gave her an awkward hug. She clenched him tightly for a moment, then released her grip. Several tears slowly slid down her cheek. Nathan whispered a strained good-bye before turning and walking away, still feeling Vannie Storm's eyes fixed upon him.

"Oh, dear me, Nathan!" she suddenly called to him. *"Jesse left this here for you!"*

Nathan spun around to respond and had to nearly catch himself from fainting. Mrs. Storm, the house, and everything else were gone. All that stood before him was rubble, just like the rest of the houses on the block.

Nathan instinctively took several steps forward, desperately, and perhaps foolishly, searching for the house and the woman he had just seen and embraced.

But it was gone... *she* was gone, and he now questioned whether she had ever been there at all. Nathan walked back up to what would have been the front doorstep and looked down.

There at his feet were two old-style computer memory cards.

Nathan reached down and picked them up. The first read:

DOMINION

Jonathan Corban Storm — Thoughts

And the second:

The Phoenix — Risen Son

11

i

Sawlus drove slowly through the town of Pittsford and pulled into the parking lot of what had apparently once been St. Louis Catholic Church. The entire structure was in disrepair, covered in graffiti and by all appearances, abandoned. Sawlus reflected momentarily on how this building, when seized from the Christian Church, was probably considered beyond usage for another philanthropic organization. Yet she was certain that this was where she needed to be.

She was emotionally drained and still carried an all-consuming sense of guilt, just waiting to be let loose, over the abandoning of her son. Her hand had stopped bleeding in the past few days, yet continued to throb. In a strange way, however, she did not mind; it was, in a sense, the last real connection she had to Caleb.

Sawlus parked her car, stepped from it, and approached the double doors entering into the church. Upon reaching the doors, she took a deep breath as she grasped the handle and pulled.

She immediately saw a priest and a young African-American man standing up at the altar. The young man, whose back was turned, immediately looked up, as if he *sensed* her, and turned in her direction. His emerald green eyes met hers, and Sawlus felt her eyes tear up.

Father Daniel, also with his back to her as he labored diligently at the altar, looked up to see Phineas, and then turned towards Sawlus. His eyes brightened with recognition.

"You have come," he stated in a tone which seemed to reflect *relief.*

Sawlus stood motionless, unable to speak, move, or even fully reflect on what was transpiring.

Father Daniel looked curiously at her as he stepped in her direction. "What is the matter, my child?"

"She cannot speak," a voice from the side came forth, startling Sawlus. It was an older man with an unkempt beard in a white cassock, strangely familiar to her, who spoke as he also approached. "It is her penance, and for now, her cross to bear."

Phineas looked confused. "*Kisa?* Surely, Enoch… she spoke as soon as she came in."

Enoch, Father Daniel, and Sawlus looked curiously at him. "She did not say a thing," the priest affirmed.

"*Wi*, she did… she said, 'I'm looking for a man called Ananias.'"

Father Daniel and Enoch exchanged glances, and an expression of understanding came across Enoch's face. "You can read her thoughts, my son."

Phineas turned to Sawlus and smiled in a slightly embarrassed fashion. "*Wi*, I suppose I can," and then looking at Sawlus he said, "Yes, I'm afraid I'm the 'Dark man' your son spoke of. I'm sorry for… for my role in how that all turned out."

Sawlus looked to him with a sense of sad affection.

"Thank you for trying to help my son."

ASCENSION

"*Mais,* it is clear now that it wasn't enough," Phineas responded.

"I take it," Father Daniel carefully cut in, "that the fact that the boy is not here means that he has chosen against joining you."

Sawlus nodded sadly.

"That must be our first task then," Enoch stated. "To retrieve the boy. He is too critical in the plan of *Elohim* to permit becoming further enveloped by the darkness."

Sawlus suddenly found herself staring intently at the man they called Enoch. He looked back at her, then over to Phineas.

"What is it?" he inquired. "She appears distressed."

Phineas looked uncomfortably back to Enoch. "She says that you are one of the *Dishalăk.*"

With that, Enoch's concerned looked faded into a gentle smile. "My child, your mind has been filled with ancient lies and newly created myths. I am a Witness of the Latter Days Come... and I will anoint you in the confirming sacrament, that you may accept your birthright as one who has been begotten from above!"

ii

Nathan sat across the desk from Carl Woodward, chief executive officer of *The Alternative,* a now near-underground publishing company with what one might call 'Christian tendencies'.

"I must say, it is quite an honor to meet the great Nathaniel Freeman-Page," Woodward shared. "Did you really think that I... or anyone for that matter... wouldn't recognize you? Even with the lame disguise?"

Nathan's face flushed.

"I kind of like the name, though... Jonathan Storm... is that a penname you use?"

"Please," Nathan interrupted. "I'm sorry, it's just that... well... discretion is of the utmost concern to me."

Woodward leaned forward over his desk. "Trust me, Mr. Freeman, discretion... along with prayer... is the only thing we think of these days."

"I appreciate that, and I appreciate you meeting with me."

"Well, I have to admit, it was quite unusual to receive your transmission. I don't know why I even paid your particular communication any mind—we get thousands of them each month. Though it wouldn't surprise me if most are phony setups from members of The Way."

"So then, what did you think of the material?"

"Did you write these?"

"No, well, yes... well... the prose is all Jonathan's... as well as the lyrics reading the songs. I only participated in the writing of the music, though I would still say that was mostly Jonathan's as well."

"It's quite good, I'd say... urgent, yet comforting in a strange way. Who exactly is Jonathan Storm?"

"An old friend. He was... he was killed in an accident before any of this was ever able to be released."

Woodward's expression transformed momentarily, as it was clear he was wrestling with a fleeting idea. "You realize that if we used your name, we'd sell a million downloads in the first day."

"No, that is not possible."

"Contractual agreements?"

"It's complicated."

Woodward nodded in acquiescence. He loved the business... he loved his recaptured Christian faith. It had been a difficult few years since the violent death of his boss and mentor, Hugh Jennings Lang, but he sensed that God had something else that He still required of him.

"Well, Mr. Freeman, my people have looked over all of these pieces of free-form prose, and are excited at the prospect of publishing this work. I think the music has promise as well."

Nathan nodded, his heart rate increasing slightly.

"I guess then we'll just leave it to the agents to work out the details, and I'll be—"

"No," Nathan interrupted. "No agents."

Woodward looked at him curiously. "You wish to negotiate a means of compensation yourself?"

ASCENSION

Nathan shook his head again. "No, Mr. Woodward. I'm not looking to be paid for this. In fact, I'm not even looking for recognition. Just a commitment from you that you'll publish these poems… the music too… *especially* the music, and do your damnedest to get them out to as many people as possible."

Woodward hesitated before looking at Nathan somewhat suspiciously. He pondered a thought for a moment, then spoke again. "Forgive me, Mr. Freeman, but I have to ask. How do I know you're not part of a plot from that crazy cult trying to catch me in a plagiarism lawsuit? I mean, I deal with that bunch every day, and they'd just love a reason to 'legitimately' close me down… and you… a member of Mystic Realism's central band…" Woodward paused for a moment. "Let me see your hand, if you would please."

Nathan felt a cold sweat break out across his body. But before he could think of what to do, Woodward came around the desk and yanked Nathan's right hand up to his face. Nathan waited for whatever was to happen next, but instead of the expected response, Carl Woodward held a look of embarrassment on his face.

"I'm sorry… I need to apologize to you." Woodward intoned as he moved back to his seat. "It's just that it's getting harder and harder to run a-an outfit not explicitly associated with The Way these days."

Nathan was nothing short of astonished. He attempted to casually look down at the back of his right hand, and to his surprise he saw that the Seal was not visible. An instant later, however, he did see it briefly glow, then fade, as did the fang marks where he had been bitten in the vision some time ago.

"So I've learned to become a bit more careful… Mr. Freeman… Mr. Freeman?"

Nathan looked back up, snapping out of his brief reverie. "I'm sorry," he apologized. "You were saying?"

Woodward gave out a mildly frustrated sigh. "What I'm saying to you, sir, is that… sure, I'll publish these poems, perhaps the music as well, and under whatever conditions you have. But first, you have to tell me the story of Jonathan Storm…"

iii

Elijah sat quietly before the committee, which he knew would take it upon themselves to end his season of civic service once and for all. Avera Kaifess, perhaps his most staunch political adversary within the Nation of Israel, addressed him as Chairman of the Commission of Inquiry.

"And would you care to explain to this commission, Mr. Lige, exactly what you were thinking when you dissented from this decree... a decree that offers the Nation of Israel *all* that it has ever asked for?"

Elijah responded, "You must beware of this Trojan Horse, Kaifess, for it asks more than it offers. It demands that Israel become a full member of the Global Communion."

"Unfortunately for you, Mr. Lige, that is not how I, nor the rest of the commission views this most gracious offer. We can only thank the Almighty that enough of the G.C. member-states looked with favor on us to ratify this decree... full membership is *not* perceived as an impediment to us. If anything, it now assures Israel a permanent and powerful place in the world community."

Elijah shook his head, and raising his voice stated. "You are playing right into the hands of our adversary. You would make an eternal deal with Satan himself to satisfy a temporal desire, one that will manifest itself in the wages of sin, which is death! It will spell the demise of us all if we accept!"

Kaifess looked to the other members of the commission, and recognizing she had their full support, continued on, overtly indignant.

"You have finally shown your true colors, Christian. The rebuilding of the Temple will provide the Jewish people a symbolic step in being reborn as a people of faith. But you are not, and have never been, a Jew at heart... even in spite of your silly masquerade as the Prophet Elijah, which in and of itself would be sufficient to have you deposed." At that moment, Kaifess took one final opportunity to make eye contact with the remaining members of the commission. She then returned her gaze to Elijah. "I see no need to go on with this inquiry as your own words have proven you guilty of treason."

Elijah looked up to Kaifess, stunned by the degree to which this inquiry had gone. He attempted to look to the other commission members for support, but they avoided his gaze, satisfied to shuffle through the papers before them.

"Still, this commission is not without compassion. You will be spared the prescribed sentence—which mind you, Mr. Lige, is to be put to death—and you will instead be relieved of your post and banished from the Nation of Israel for the rest of your days. If you choose to return, the full sentence will be imposed."

12

Peace of mind
Peace of heart
Pieces of a dream
Which still elude me

A shadowed past,
Or empathic vision?
I continue to seek
Albeit reluctantly
The key to this portentous door

The Child
Though harmed
Is now safe
Yearning to heal
Yet still
Driving away
The very souls
Who greatly desire to tend his wounds

A fortress has been built
To protect this Little Prince
From He that rejected the child
He that failed him
When Love
Was most needed
Most sought
Most lacking

DOMINION

This castle
Though grand and mighty
Has become his prison.

The bridge is drawn
Its moat is deep
And its walls are high

All that escapes
Is the delicate sound
Of a grief-stricken boy
Weeping—

      "I have nothing left!"

So now
As the drawbridge begins its descent
I must ask myself;

      Will I have the courage
      To face this child
      Whom I so absently
      Yet still
      Knowingly
      Sentenced to death?

– Jonathan Corban Storm
Royal Negligence

i

"I just can't believe she would do it... I mean, we're talking the Iron Queen here!" Siro Scribner stated in utter disbelief.

"Perhaps the company she kept was not sufficiently supportive of her strong beliefs," responded Tæsír Hoc.

Siro glared at him in anger. "What the hell's that supposed to mean?"

"Please," the Prophet responded. "It was no secret that she was unsatisfied with you as her *Breha*. As an editor, you are the best, of that I have no question. But as a man of The Way... and, I might add, as a *man* period, you are grossly lacking."

"I don't have to listen to this!" Siro retorted, rising from his seat and moving towards the door. "I've had Brother Kako on this trail since she disappeared, and he has not come up with any of what you are saying."

"And what of your little traitor friend?"

Siro stopped at the door and spun around. "What the hell are you talking about?"

"Nathaniel. I believe the two of you were... close."

Siro took a few steps back towards Tæsír Hoc. "Yeah, what about it?"

The Prophet sighed patronizingly. "Well, it seems Jimi T. had given the fool a simple task, and he chose to blatantly defy him and go off on his own merry way. It has been three months, and no one has heard a word from him."

Siro was dumbfounded. "Why was I not informed of this?"

Tæsír Hoc shrugged. "I am not sure. I suppose as he was your friend, it would not be presumptuous to assume you would know first."

"Well, I didn't," Siro remarked angrily.

"Tsk, tsk... please do not become hostile, young Siro, as it gets better. The cretin hooked himself up with a publication—one that tries to hide its true nature, but that is nonetheless *Christian*. They are set to publish a series of poems written by a fool who's been dead for more than seven years."

Siro felt a sinking feeling in his stomach. "So what is Jimi T. going to do about him?"

The Prophet shrugged his shoulders and shook his head. "Nothing for the moment—he is more concerned about the woman. If she is to contact you, you must inform me immediately. A fallen member of The Way is a danger to both herself and other believers. She must not be allowed to destroy what we have so painstakingly built!"

DOMINION

ii

Annie D. Nesterov sat quietly in her small apartment in South Philadelphia. After her experience at the autobus station, inspiring her to stay on in this city, she had chosen a dwelling within walking distance of her beloved St. Maximilian Kolbe Blessed Sacrament Chapel. Unfortunately, the F.A.I.R. Act had closed it down, and it now served as a youth center for Mystic Realism's *Ñeo Místè*.

A scandal it is! I see, dear Mother, that your weepin' is for good reason!

She had kept her life simple from that day, only furnishing her apartment with a table, a chair, and a mat on which to sleep. The simplicity had provided a certain sense of interior healing for her, to the degree that she could now embrace her past—with sadness, certainly, but also incorporating a profound sense of understanding. God had permitted her afflictions, even those that found their origin outside of her own choices.

She had suffered much, and now she loved much.

There was a knock at her door.

"Mrs. Nesterov? It is me, Matt Kohl. Are you home?"

Annie D.'s heart leapt. The young seminarian regularly visited her several times a week. He was only a month away from being ordained a deacon, and she could not be more proud. He had become like a son to her.

Annie opened the door to find the smiling young man wearing a coat which could not hide his Roman collar. Her anxiety shot up, knowing that the amendment to the F.A.I.R. Act permitting seminarians and deacons to remain in the North American Union was expected to be rescinded this week.

"My God, Matthew! You'll be gettin' on with the authorities by not hidin' your collar! Get in here before you bring down the wrath of the government on us!"

Matthew smiled and winked as he embraced Annie and entered the apartment. He was about to speak when he suddenly looked around the room and gasped.

"Mrs. Nesterov! What have you done with the place?"

Annie D. smiled as she closed the door. It was clear that the young man was referring to the two-dozen or so framed pictures up on the once bare walls.

96

ASCENSION

"Well, I was figurin' it was time to bring me family out. To be true, it was a wee bit too painful to see them until now."

Matthew seemed mesmerized as he moved over to the photographs, entering into the one dimension of Annie D.'s being she had never shared with him. He moved along the wall until he came upon a certain image and suddenly stopped.

"Mrs. Nesterov, I know the two boys in this picture. Jonathan and Nathan, I went to high school with them. We were friends until…"

Annie D.'s eyes began to fill up as the young seminarian looked back at her. His eyes suddenly widened as he realized his insensitivity.

"Ohh, Mrs. Nesterov, I'm sorry… you were… they were…"

"The boy, the one you're callin' Jonathan, he was me grandson. His real name was Jesse. He had lived a… a troubled life, you would say."

Matthew looked down. "Yes… I was there when it happened. I am sorry. He was a good person, and I know his faith was important to him."

"Aye," Annie D. breathed, but with a slightly happier tone. "That is my sole consolation in losin' the boy. He's with the good Lord, of that I'm sure."

Matthew paused for a moment, and it became clear he had come for more than just a social visit.

"I am sorry, Mrs. Nesterov, I don't have much time today. I came to tell you that I am leaving."

Annie D.'s eyes widened. "Leavin'? Dear boy, you're only a tick away from becomin' a deacon! Are ya leavin' your vocation?"

Matthew lifted his hands in a reassuring gesture. "No! Certainly not. It is only that God has revealed to me a more specific dimension of my calling. I will be leaving in three days for the Bronx for my ordination, and then I'm going to be sent down to Comayagua, Honduras. I'm going to be a Franciscan Friar!"

"Praise Jesus!" Annie D. exclaimed, then a moment later she was unable to cover her slight sense of sadness… even loss. "I'll not be seein' you again then, will I?"

Matthew stepped closer to Annie, who had still not moved away from the front door of her apartment. "Well, that is part of what I wanted to speak to you about, Mrs. Nesterov—"

"There's handle on my jug, luv. Will you ever learn to call me Annie?"

Matthew smiled. "Well, with God, all things are possible. But in seriousness, I strongly believe that it is time that you take Father Daniel up on his offer. I've prayed about it, Annie, and in truth, I have a clear sense that something big is about to happen—something both wonderful and terrible, but in the end, necessary. I don't believe you are supposed to stay here."

Annie D. felt the blood drain from her face. She had just begun to make a home of this place, but there was something in what the young seminarian was saying that rang true in her heart. She looked down uncomfortably, then walked over to the picture of Jesse and Nathan. She pulled it off the wall, gazing at the grandson she barely got to know in his shortened lifetime.

Is this where you're leadin' me, Jesse? I've felt your presence… I'm certain of it. Now you've brought your old friend to me. It's Providence, I'm sure. I just don't know when to hold fast, and when to let go.

She turned to Matthew. "I've sensed this 'somethin' big' that you speak about as well… just wasn't sure of my part in it all. So my question to you is, when do I leave?"

His expression was clearly one of relief. "I took the liberty, after speaking with Father Daniel, of purchasing you a ticket on the autobus. It leaves a week from today. Phinny will meet you… as you know, Father Daniel is in hiding, and it seems that the way things are going, Phinny will be as well."

"Yes, a wicked time we're livin' in when a priest can't show his face."

Matthew nodded in solemn acknowledgement. After a moment passed, he spoke again. "There is one more thing I wanted to speak to you about."

There was a long pause, which Annie D. did not permit to grow any longer. "Well, go on then, boy. It's clear as day now that we don't have all the time in the world!"

Matthew chuckled. "I needed… I needed to speak to you about a little boy. His name is Felipe…"

iii

Nathan sat on the bed in the cheap motel room that Woodward had obtained for him. Despite his near-unlimited resources when in came to money, he was afraid to permit a palm or retinal scan to be taken, knowing that he would potentially be traced by Jimi T.'s men. He wasn't even certain that the Mystic King would have a problem with what he was doing, but he had essentially gone AWOL on the mission he had been given by the one who called him 'my rock'.

So he spent most of his time in this small dive of a motel in Perth Amboy, New Jersey, reading (Woodward had found him some quite intriguing old books on philosophy) resting, and trying to recover whatever spark he could muster of that old passion for life—or at least for survival.

Tonight, he had seen many dressed as ghouls and goblins running in the streets. It seemed Halloween was the only holiday of the past which people still celebrated. In fact, its prominence had even grown, with the majority of adults even entering into the trick-or-treat "fun."

Nathan shook his head gently as he pulled out his old acoustic guitar, lay back on the bed, and began to pluck an arpeggio while trying to make sense of it all.

What am I doing?

13

i

Phineas looked across the inside of the van and reached out to give Sawlus a reassuring pat on the leg. The trouble was, it was really he that needed reassuring.

"I have a bad feeling about this, Phinny."

Sawlus had been on a "high" for the past two months, first watching her Seal simply wash off in the holy water during her Sacrament of Confirmation, and then, learning to be a Christian once again, this time, by her own choice. She was further encouraged, even intrigued, by another woman who had arrived to join the crew only a few weeks ago. This woman was older, and clearly maternal, but Sawlus had not yet found the manner in which to approach her. The woman, called 'Annie', would spend most of her day in front of the Blessed Sacrament in prayer. It was comforting to Sawlus to know that is where she was at this very moment.

I wonder where my own mother is...

Phineas looked momentarily confused, not able to read Sawlus' inner thoughts, though still sensing the struggle. He shook his head and feigned a smile, responding to her comment directed towards him with a whisper. "Oh1 *sha sha*, Sawlus. There's nothing to worry about. We'll be in and out with Caleb before anyone knows what hit them."

Father Daniel looked back from the passenger seat, still not having grown accustomed to hearing only one side of the conversation between the two. "We're only a few blocks away. Are you ready for this, Phinny?"

Phineas took a deep breath and nodded his head. "I'm ready."

"Okay," the former police officer and ex-Navy Seal Bud Petrall began from the driver's side. He had arrived to join the small band only the week before. "Once you're in, we'll create the diversion that should separate the adults from the children. We won't have much time, so hit Caleb with the tranquilizer, and get him out of there any way you can. You'll have our people waiting at three separate points."

"*Mo Konmprann,*" Phineas responded absently, not fully paying attention. He looked up to see the perplexed expression in the rearview mirror by Bud. "Ahh… I am sorry, I understand."

He had to admit, he was excited at the prospect of utilizing some of his old, antisocial skills to glorify the work of his God. He was confident he could be in and out of the house without even so much as an insect knowing what had happened.

Bud made one last turn in the opposite direction of their destination, then flipped on the scrambler, which would make them essentially invisible to the global positioning system for a short period, before secondary land-based towers would be alerted to the absence of a signal.

"Okay, this is it," Father Daniel stated as the van pulled across the street. "Let's join hands."

The four of them did as instructed. Father Daniel led them in a brief prayer, then provided the entire group with a blessing.

"Amen," the others responded at the close of the blessing. None seemed to experience much solace following the prayer, but considering the circumstances, none were seeking any either.

Phineas exchanged looks with each of them, then smiled coyly and slipped out the van door.

He was pleased to find that his skills had not diminished in the slightest. In less than ninety seconds, he had scaled the wall, picked a lock on the second-story window, and entered the house.

Their sources had informed them that a small get-together of parents and members of the *Nèo Mstè* was to take place at this home, and that Caleb would be present. Phineas felt his heart beat with excitement as he peered out into the hallway.

He heard adults speaking as well as children's laughter. He crept to the top of the stairway and looked down.

"Hey, Holmes."

Phineas nearly jumped out of his skin. There, standing in the darkness at the other end of the hallway, was a young boy of perhaps ten or eleven years. With his face still in the shadows, the figure began to move towards him.

"You got somethin' for me, yo?"

Phineas stood, frozen, yet still puzzled at the familiarity of the boy. He could now discern the fact that this child was also African-American, and despite his street language, there was a discernable touch of an accent. It was...

"*Kisa?* What do you mean?" Phineas inquired in a half-whisper.

The boy became annoyed. "I said, muthafucka, you got somethin' for me, yo?"

The boy held his hand in a position familiar to Phineas, underneath his shirt, perhaps packing a gun, perhaps not.

"Do I know you?" Phineas asked, starting to look around in case of the need for a quick exit.

"You gonna know me and forget me real soon, yo. Time you recognize, fool."

And with that, the youth stepped into the light, and Phineas' heart sank.

He was staring face to face with a young Phineas Savoie, or as he was known on the street, "Flint."

"Pretty convincing, isn't he?" a voice spoke out from behind him.

Phineas spun around as the entire scene seemed to spin itself in the opposite direction. There was a moment of vertigo, and then he suddenly found himself standing in a large room surrounded by perhaps a dozen members of the *Nèo Mstè*. The man known as Jimi T. Expo slowly circled the outside perimeter, while the image of Flint remained inside the circle, several meters

ASCENSION

from Phineas.

"I tried to warn you... to protect you, Phineas. For I saw great potential in you."

Phineas, finding that the image of his pre-Christian days had woken up something within him, snarled back, "Potential to do your evil work?"

The Mystic King allowed a brief hint of a smile to emerge. "Are you still holding on to that, Phineas? Is your mind still so limited that it can only accept good versus evil, black versus white? You tell me, Phineas, who is better, the blacks or the whites?"

"Neither," he retorted.

The Mystic King nodded his head. "I see... and which is greater, the mountains or the valleys? The land or the sea? Man or woman?"

Phineas tried to shake his head free, to ignore the crooked logic which was being set upon him.

"In battle, each nation always believes that it is *they* that are in the right. Both sides pray to your god for victory. But whose prayers will he answer?"

"I..."

"It's a matter of perspective, most would say, my son, but I'm afraid it's even more than that. It's a matter of *respect* for another's beliefs. Should you not be free to pray to your god, and I to mine? Can one simply be left, and the other, right? Can not the two poles co-exist?"

Phineas struggled. "There is but one truth!"

Jimi T. paused, cocking his head. "Is there, my boy? Can you really be certain of that? And for that matter, can you really be sure of any of this?"

Phineas shook his head, his mind beginning to swim.

"You came here to violate the free will of a young boy. Free will... that's a principle of your higher power, *and* mine. Now I am prepared to let you walk out that door and for us all to continue to express our freedoms in whichever way we choose. I have no war with you, nor do I wish to."

Phineas looked around him, a dozen youthful eyes situated in clean-shaven heads fixed upon his face, awaiting his answer. He looked at the image of himself in his younger years, which began to blur and change. The boy's skin lightened, his size shortened, and in a moment, Phineas was looking at a brightly smiling Caleb.

"I know you have tried to help me, Phinny. And for that, I love you. Come with us and be my brother. We can make a bit of heaven right here on Earth."

Phineas felt the warmth and affection coming from this boy... a boy he *had* loved. A boy he *still* loved...

"Think of it, young Phineas." Jimi T. again spoke. "Which side is it that really wants to annihilate the other anyway? And what exactly does the destruction of another have to do with loving thy neighbor?"

A million thoughts and emotions swept through Phineas' head as a single tear broke free from his tear duct.

"I... I..."

"Phinny! Where are you?"

The spell broke, and Phineas looked upon Jimi T. with an expression that was quickly read by the Mystic King.

"You sad... sad... fool...I only desired to help," Jimi T. breathed.

As if to complete this horrible dream, the shadowed feminine figure from his previous vision once again became manifest, standing silently in the corner.

Phineas reached into his shirt for the tranquilizer, but suddenly found that he had lost the ability to control his body. It shook as if a million volts ran through it, and he fell to his knees before Caleb. The room swiftly darkened, and was now filled with a myriad of lit candles. Only the four individuals remained.

"I so much wished for you to be my friend," Caleb spoke. "But you would not be this for me. It is your wish to control me, not to help me grow."

"I am afraid it is too late for talk, my son. It is time for penance," the Mystic King stated gravely.

"Yes, Abba. As you say."

Phineas looked on in horror as the shadowed figure stepped into the flickering light.

"*Se konsa!* Dis be da truth. I told you, boy, you are *my* seed, and you'll not be defyin' me."

A soul-piercing scream emerged from inside the house as Sawlus instantly reached for her temples, then slumped to the floor of the van, unconscious. Father Daniel and Bud looked at each other momentarily before jumping out of the vehicle and sprinting towards the front door.

Surprisingly, the several guards were now gone, and Bud was barely slowed as he kicked through the side door to the building. Father Daniel followed immediately, and then froze. He and Bud were now staring at the same disturbing sight.

They moved forward, slowly, up to Phineas Savoie, whose body lay, feet together and arms extended, on the floor before them. His eye sockets were burned straight through to the back of the skull, and he had the Seal of Mystic Realism carved into his chest.

"This c-cannot b-be!" Father Daniel stammered, not accepting that which lay before him. "He was one of the Christian Elect... it was not yet his time!"

ii

"Listen, you told me you would publish these! I've been laid up in this rat hole for almost three months. I'm going to go crazy if I'm here for much longer."

Nathan was clearly frustrated with Carl Woodward. Even though the soon-to-be publisher of Jonathan's work came to visit at least four or five times a week, the isolation was becoming more than Nathan could handle.

Carl nodded sympathetically, looking around the small rundown motel room. "I can understand that, Nathan. My funds are a bit limited—I'm working with government agents in investigating why I have not received my monthly checks from them in nearly a year. At the moment, I'm living off the generosity of others myself. But I can try to see if I can get you whatever you need."

Nathan shook his head. "No, I don't need anything more. I don't *deserve* anything more. Can't I do just one transaction from my account to yours... then be done with it?"

But Carl shook his head. "Not a good idea. If these people are looking for you, they're keeping a close eye on all of your assets. It was your idea to keep our relationship completely anonymous as far as the rest of the world was concerned, and with recent events, I see the wisdom in that even more."

"I'm not exactly sure, Carl, why I even care about them finding me. I just... I just feel like I'm on the verge of a clarity that has eluded me my entire life. I'm not ready to go back... not yet. Maybe once Jonathan's stuff is out there, I can feel I've done what I need to do."

"Really, Nathan, I can put you up with some friends of mine who are good at minding their own business."

"*Christian* friends?"

Carl provided an exasperated nod of acknowledgement.

"Then no thanks, Carl. I said I'm on the verge of clarity, and the last thing I want is someone selling me *their* beliefs on anything. I'm not a fool... I know your publishing house is a thinly disguised Christian group—but really, I could care less. I have no doubt it was what Jes— err, Jonathan would have wanted."

Carl nodded. "Understood. Yet the offer still remains, and I promise no sales techniques."

Nathan's expression made his approval evident. "So when are you going to publish?"

Carl maintained a steady expression as he looked at Nathan. "I hope you appreciate that timing is everything in this, Nathan, even if we had the money. I've been in the communications and media business for some time—and I am also a man of prayer... at least now I am. So you are going to have to trust me on this one. There is something big coming up... I can sense it, and those around me feel the same. I believe it will be both great and terrible at the same time. When it hits—and I don't believe it will be long—it's then that we'll strike with this. I think the world will be needing something like this at that point."

iii

Joakima looked on at her firstborn son, Almon, barely ten years of age, lying on his bed with a fever that had not broken for two days. She had initially been ecstatic about returning to the homeland in preparation for the rebuilding of the Third Temple. With the return of the Ark of the Covenant to the Holy Land, as well as the blessing of the man who some now suggested to be the long awaited Messiah, it had seemed as if nothing could taint her joy.

Even more, there were now rumors that Enoch and Elijah had returned to again free their people. Though others refuted this claim, instead claiming that imposters were everywhere, seeking power to destroy the very foundations of Judaism itself.

Yet despite all these events which gave great reason for hope, something very... very *wrong* was afoot throughout their land. It seemed to have its genesis no more than a month ago, but in that time her cousin had suffered the sudden loss of her newborn baby, and now her own firstborn son was deathly ill. Joakima's uncle, the highly revered Rabbi Saul Wilson, a disciple of the Israel's high priest, Solomon Abrams, was out presiding over the funeral of another neighborhood boy, this one only six years of age. Yes... in this short time, Joakima's enthusiasm for the purported renewal of her nation and faith had become soured.

She looked up to a framed picture of the Mystic King on her wall and prayed.

"How can I put my faith in two prophets who may or may not be who they say? You are here, and you can help...now."

She hesitated, knowing that her husband, a local carpenter and devout Jew, would not approve of her actions.

"I place my child's life in your hands, oh King of Kings."

iv

Luther stood atop the pinnacle of the Third Temple. Though it had only been four months of work, it was quite clear that it would not take the prescribed three and a half years to bring it to completion. Two at most, he thought. He fought against an urge to destroy it himself right then and there, in a very obvious way demonstrating his disdain for what the Mystic King was doing. This Temple seemed to represent everything that was wrong with the *modo de proceder* of the so-called 'Anointed'.

A moment passed, and Luther was suddenly flanked by Marius and Anaxagoras.

"An intriguing view," Anaxagoras exclaimed.

"Yes," Marius responded with a wry smile. "One truly to die for..."

They both looked to the pensive Luther. "So then, Luther, why have you summoned us?" Marius inquired. "This is highly irregular, outside of the context of the full Council."

"There is much that is irregular in these days. What I have to share with each of you does not concern the others. In fact, outside of the two of you, I have found myself questioning as to whom I can trust."

Anaxagoras looked surprised, or at least titillated. "Really? Not even Cato? Eumenes?"

"Cato, despite his words, seems to be in lockstep with the Anointed. And why not? The Anointed's plan offers quite a prominent role for him in the age to come."

"And Eumenes?"

Luther's expression was one of genuine bewilderment. "I cannot be sure where his loyalties lie. His extracurricular activities seem to suggest that his primary focus is an agenda of his own making—his own personal interests."

Marius chuckled. "Do not be so certain, Luther, that any of us do not give our own interests primacy."

Luther nodded with a dry smile. "So true, my old friend. So true." He then again looked out across the whole of Jerusalem, resuming his pensive mood.

A moment later, he again spoke. "Anaxagoras, I must commend you on your virulent defense against the proposal to rebuild this temple in the G.C. meeting. Quite convincing."

"You were there?"

"In spirit."

"Well, the truth be known," Anaxagoras began. "It was not completely feigned. The Anointed continues to make my circumstances... how should I say... *difficult*. I may be old, but on this side of eternity, I am by no means immortal. If I come across as weak to any within the Islamic fold, there are many who would relish the opportunity to cut my throat and assume my place."

"Then we are in agreement."

"Of what?"

Luther stepped off the apex, but instead of falling, he remained suspended many meters above the ground, as if on solid footing. He turned to face both men.

"We can no longer remain in the position of only hoping for the best if we are not at the same time preparing for the worst. We must begin to put things in place under the possible scenario that the Anointed will not be able to consummate his calling in line with the plan of the Great Seraph."

"What are you proposing?" Anaxagoras inquired, clearly intrigued.

"Certain steps are being taken, though I will need your confidence to move forward. We are three, perhaps four months away from an incredible transformation—a clear and authentic act against the scourge of our existence. The Anointed's actions—even reactions—to this initiative will make his intentions manifest."

Anaxagoras cocked an eyebrow. "And if his response fails to align with your expectations?"

Luther turned to Marius. "The young man, he is here?"

Marius nodded. "Yes. As you requested, he was retrieved. By his father no less, at my bidding. He seems to be finding plenty of opportunity here to indulge his appetites."

"Very well," Luther responded.

"What are your plans for the man?" Anaxagoras asked, not wishing to be left in the dark on this one.

"Perhaps he will not be needed at all. But in the case he is, *Caliph*, the good *Rabbi* over here will be the first to know."

14

i

It was still several hours before dawn on the first day of the Jewish Passover. Christopher stood at the entrance to Saint Peter's Square in the Vatican, flanked on one side by Enoch, and on the other by Elijah. They had met just a day before with Father Daniel Ananias, prayed with him and provided him with an anointing for the difficult task that lay ahead. The aspired-to meeting between Father Daniel and Peter II had never materialized... it seemed that Providence either did not desire it, or had permitted its prevention. Father Daniel, still grief-stricken over the loss of young Phineas six months prior, was at this very moment being smuggled via a chartered boat to the small island of Bimini off the U.S. coast—one of the twelve Global Communion headquarters.

"We are about to enter into very dark times. Why... why is this night different than all other nights?" But Christopher's uncharacteristically shaky voice faltered. "I must confess... God's ways are sometimes mysterious beyond even a shadow of my understanding. But how can *this* be permitted to pass?"

"It has been foretold," Elijah began, his eyes fixed on the great doors to St. Peter's Basilica. "Before Christ's return, the Church must pass through a final trial that will shake the faith of many believers."

Enoch continued, as if on cue. "The persecution that accompanies Her pilgrimage on Earth will unveil the 'mystery of iniquity' in the form of a religious deception... one that we have already witnessed the genesis of, which offers humanity an apparent solution to their problems... yet at the price of apostasy from the truth."

"She must walk the same road of Calvary as did Christ, Christopher. We have all been called to do our part."

"But the sacrifice..." He then turned to each of them, almost pleading. "We have sent Daniel into the lion's den... do any of us believe his mission stands a chance of succeeding?"

Enoch breathed in deeply, releasing a sigh of understanding. "What seems unlikely to us, even impossible, still must take place. The choice *must* be given. Despite all prophecy suggesting a specific end, all have been created destined for the Father."

Christopher shook his head slowly, though not truly disagreeing with what was said. "Even him?"

"Perhaps, *especially* him."

"By now," Elijah intervened, "the Christian Elect have assembled... The Gathering has become manifest. Their intercession may very well stave off the evil of the hour."

Christopher took a deep breath himself, allowing his gaze to drift upward. "I understand neither the depths of God's permissive will, nor the ocean of His mercy. Yet I trust that His will be done."

"It is time for that which has been freely given to be freely returned."

ii

"So am I to understand, Colonel, that all those whom we have had under surveillance have reached their final destination?" Tæsír Hoc inquired.

Colonel Nick Orieton of the newly established Global Communion Peacekeeping Force bowed his head as he responded, "Yes, my lord. They, along with many others, have assembled in twelve different sites around the globe… in generally remote areas… but all apparently places of pilgrimage."

"In what regions have they gathered?"

"In Mexico, Croatia, France, Spain, Japan, Portugal, Ireland, Poland, Italy, Egypt, Rwanda, and Venezuela."

The Prophet provided a curious smile as he walked up to the full wall video map of the world. With a click, Orieton allowed the locations to be highlighted.

"How many at each location?"

"It appears to be greater than ten thousand at each… perhaps as much as twelve or thirteen."

"Has Sanger's weapon been mobilized?"

"Per your request, my lord, we have our forces in place to deploy the weapon at your command."

Tæsír Hoc walked alongside the map image, trying to put together exactly *why* those *Cørtät* who identified themselves as the 'Christian Elect' had chosen to make themselves such easy targets.

Like sheep being led to the slaughter.

He narrowed his eyes momentarily. "Can we zoom in on any location?"

"Yes, my lord."

"Then do it. Give me the location in Rwanda."

"Very well, my lord. The town is called Kibeho."

The screen zoomed in rapidly until it came to rest on the image of a large church on a plateau with heavily wooded hills sloping down each side.

ASCENSION

Thousands upon thousands of men and women were seen throughout the scene, all kneeling.

"What are they doing?" the Prophet inquired, his disgust evident.

"I believe they are praying, my lord."

Tæsír Hoc let out a disgusted chortle. "How quaint." Then with a quick turn, he looked back at Orieton. "Have your men prepare for weapon deployment at all locations on my word."

Orieton hesitated, apparently somewhat uncomfortable. "My lord?"

"Is there a problem, Colonel? Please do not tell me you do not have the stomach for this..."

"No... it is not that, my lord... only that... does it not require the authorization of the Sovereign to engage the enemy?"

"I should hope, Colonel, that my authorization is sufficient for you. . especially if you have aspirations of a much higher post. But if you must know, the Mystic King is well aware of this operation, though it is expedient for him to not be involved. They call it, 'plausible deniability'. Though some... perhaps myself included... may refer to it as plausible cowardice..."

iii

Mikhail laughed loudly as he downed his seventh shot of Tequila at the upscale *discothèque* in the heart of the city of Comayagua, Honduras. While most in the tiny nation were fasting in anticipation of the Easter celebration, he was still able to scare up several hundred locals who wished to celebrate his final closing of a deal with the Honduran drug lords, completing his total monopoly over organized crime in Central and South America.

"Vive Honduras!" he shouted out, holding shot number eight in the air, to the cheers of the many who were celebrating off his tab. He took it down in no more than a second, then drew his cigarette to his mouth, inhaling deeply. He suddenly broke into a coughing fit, yet it was clear to him, if not everyone else around him, that it was not a simple tickle of the throat.

As he leaned over and pulled the handkerchief from his pocket, the mariachi band began to play, and all those around him turned to focus on more festive things. Mikhail continued to cough deeply as he brought the handkerchief to his mouth. A minute or so later, the coughing stopped, and he pulled away the handkerchief, which was now covered in bloodspots. He had ignored the pleas of his doctor regarding his alleged lung cancer for more than two years now, claiming that he "felt great." Though especially in the past month, despite his successes at his many negotiations, Mikhail could no longer kid himself as to the state of his health.

I guess I should not put this off much longer... though we all have to die someday.

He looked to the bartender. "Hey, Marcos, can I bum another cigarette?"

15

The Signs of the Times
<<n 3.282>>

THE VATICAN — Previously unsubstantiated reports were confirmed today regarding the sexual misconduct of Peter II, head of the Christian Church.

Incriminating photos were released this morning showing the Pontiff, then Monsignor Pietro Columba, engaging in sexual relations with at least nine different young boys, ranging in age from seven to fifteen.

Each of the identified boys, now adults, have participated in the investigation over the past three years, and it is believed that as many as two-dozen additional former altar servers will come forth with further statements of abuse at the hands of the Pontiff, prior to his election to his current post.

Peter was unavailable for comment this morning, but it is expected that Vatican police will take him into custody sometime within the next 48 hours.

DOMINION

i

It had been a grueling journey, but Father Daniel had made sure that he spent most of it resting, fasting, and praying. Though he would never permit a prideful thought to pass his mind unhindered, he did feel that he was in the best frame of spirit he could have hoped to be. Bud Petrall had brought him to within a hundred meters of the 'target' facility. The last part, he would do on his own.

It was still at least thirty minutes before sunrise on the island of Bimini. With a final prayer to himself, reflecting on the near hundred and fifty thousand men and women who were interceding for him at this very moment—not to mention the great multitude in heaven—he slipped over the wall and into the back door, which he was assured would be unlocked. It was.

Father Daniel saw a light coming from an open door down the hallway. It was the door to the room he had been informed about. Trying not to be heard, he moved stealthily down the hall, then entered the open room.

The Mystic King stood with his back to the priest, looking through a book pulled from a vast library. He sensed someone had entered, and spoke.

"Reba, I would prefer that you knock when you—" he suddenly turned, locking eyes with Father Daniel.

"Well, I must say, this is quite a ... surprise."

Father Daniel was heartened. He had never seen the one revered by so many as "The Anointed" apparently caught off-guard. Yet at this moment, it would seem for the first time in the Mystic King's life, something had not gone exactly according to plan.

"I would have thought," Jimi T. began, seemingly having fully regained his composure, "that a Christian priest would be the last person on Earth to request an audience with me. To whom do I have the pleasure of speaking?"

"I am Father Daniel Ananias, and I come to share with you tidings of great joy."

◊◊◊

ASCENSION

"Deploy the first stage of the weapon," Tæsír Hoc directed.

"By your command, my lord."

◊◊◊

Peter II stood from his seat and ambled slowly towards the window. He positioned himself just to the left of it, peering carefully down into Saint Peter's Square.

The angry shouts rose up towards him as tens of thousands released their outrage, hurling rocks towards the window. They were not shouting for his death—they were demanding his crucifixion.

He had known that this time would come. A final meeting with Christopher, Enoch, and Elijah had provided some form of consolation, yet still, he had not expected his final demise to come about quite like this. Peter's soul had plunged deep into the dark night only a day before, and he no longer felt the Spirit move within him as it once had. His brilliant radiance, practically visible to the outside observer in his heyday, now seemed to be reduced to a dwindling flicker.

His body was now covered with miserable sores, both inside and out, not unlike those of his brother in Christ, Andreas II. He fought against the wretched void which slowly attempted to envelop his heart, seeking to inject its ooze of despair, and its seeds of doubt.

Peter felt a new sensation grip him… one that had not touched his soul for many years. He was *afraid.*

He looked to heaven and got down, with considerable difficulty, on his knees. "Father, You have always spoken to me so clearly. I realize that what is to happen must happen… though I do wish this cup to be passed from me." A twinge in his stomach grew stronger as his breath grew more shallow and hurried. "But, Abba, I did not know that I would feel abandoned in my time of need. Forgive me in my weakness… forgive me in my doubt."

He began to weep, but quickly tried to pull himself together. This was the Father's will. He would stake his immortal soul on it.

Peter winced as he stood and then moved towards the phone, attempting to contact the head of the Swiss Guard in order to get a better sense of the situation. He was not surprised to find that the phone was dead. He looked towards the door, hesitated momentarily, then moved towards it.

Opening the door, the ailing Pontiff peered out into the hallway.

"Hello?" he called out.

But there was no response save the echo of his own unsteady voice.

"Anyone?" he shouted. "Is there anyone there?"

This time he heard a slight rustle from around the corner.

"Who is that? Monsignor Ebright?"

Suddenly, a voice called out from within the room, behind him.

"Feeling a bit lonely, Peter?"

The Pope, startled, spun around and slammed the door all in one motion. His eyes struggled to instantly focus on the figure that had somehow slipped into his room.

Full recognition took only a moment.

"Dear God…" he whispered to himself.

The slightest trace of a curious smile emerged from the face of this ghost-like man, a dull glow emanating from him. There in his room with him was none other than his predecessor, Leo XIV.

"You seem surprised, Peter, but I would have expected the Holy See to have had enlightened you on my planned demise."

Peter took a hesitant step towards Leo, trying to establish for himself if what he was seeing was indeed real.

"You died, Leo. Your plane disappeared. They sent out a search party—"

"Oh, no *real* search party was ever sent, Peter," Leo interrupted. "You do not send a search party after something you have intended to lose."

Peter looked confused. "What do you mean? Why would anyone—?"

"Please, Peter, your ignorance is beginning to disgust me. You are still completely oblivious to many of the things I set in motion while serving as the Pontiff of this wholly pathetic religion."

Peter tried not to wince at the words his predecessor spoke.

"I went to great lengths to conceal my true nature, my true identity, and my true purpose. Not even your two precious Witnesses were aware of my plans. Still, someone, somehow found out, and it was at that time that my assassination was planned."

Peter looked shocked. "Assassination?"

Again, that trace of a smile emerged, contrasting sharply with Leo's stone-cold eyes.

"That is correct, and it would not have been the first in our shared line, yes Peter? But unfortunately for these poor, misled fellows, one cannot easily kill that which is no longer fully mortal. My days of mortality ended near two millennia ago on the Isle of Atlantis. It was there that I accepted my destiny, as one of the chosen... as one of the *Illumini*."

Peter's eyes widened, and he found himself speechless. At that moment, a stone crashed through the window and seemingly passed right through Leo, falling to the ground. The shouts could be heard clearly now, and it seemed that the rage had heightened.

"Leo..."

"No, that name is no longer applicable, at least for you, my friend. You may call me by my true name. It is I... the great Cato!"

And with that, a full sinister smile emerged which reeked of pure evil.

Peter suddenly felt a strange... yet welcome... sense of resolution fill his spirit. "What is it you intend to do, Leo?"

"Not just I, my friend, and not just what we *intend* to do, but what we *have* done. Centuries ago, we discovered the path to eternity. For generations we have worked in the shadows, whispering in the ears of men of power—men of *promise*—they were all too willing to be pawns in our end game. In a mere twelve generations, we have transformed humanity in preparation for the coming age. Only now—in this generation—have we stepped onto center stage to bring to full fruition that which we set in motion long ago. We have infiltrated every dismal religion and have risen to the highest ranks in each. Truly, it was pathetic how easy it was! Your followers have itchy ears for any message that excuses their transgressions or channels and justifies their wrath. They are drowning in their own putrid pool of mediocrity."

Peter looked steadily at the man called Cato. He had been in the presence of corrupted good before, but not to this degree. Cato continued.

"And you know what was really most amusing to us, Peter? It is that these stupid sheep have been fattened, sheared, and are skipping happily to the slaughter. Near all of your leaders have been complicit; truly, we could not have done it without them!"

Peter absorbed the diatribe, yet with each vile statement made by this near-immortal, he actually felt the strength of God returning to him.

"Leo, your pride has clouded your reason, and your betrayal of humanity will not go without a final accounting. Still, this is *your* time… a season of darkness which we have not seen in two thousand years. Do what you have come to do…"

◊◊◊

"So, Father, do you really believe you can talk me out of what I claim to believe?"

The Mystic King seemed almost tickled.

"No, I do not. Anything someone can be talked into, they can be talked out of. What I ask of you, what I offer you, is a choice."

With that, Jimi T. was unable to fully restrain a laugh. "Perhaps it is *you*, dear Priest, who suffers from a wealth of pride. Can you tell me at what point I was given a choice?"

"We all have an intellect and a will, and we have the ability to choose to love He that *is* love, or to reject that love."

"Really, Priest? Did not your god create me? Did he not know me 'in my mother's womb?' Did he not desire me to play a specific… *opposing* part in his silly game?"

"His knowledge of events, past and future, does not require the suspension of our free will."

"Does it not? It would seem to me that it does. But be that as it may, Priest, what do you propose? That I bow down before a fettering dead god? Truly, Christianity has failed to liberate mankind. Where is the promise of His coming? Look at the world! It has not grown better in the past two millennia, it has grown worse… until now!"

Though the arguments proposed were not new to Father Daniel, these words still seemed to carry a seductive, unsettling air to them. "What man sees in time, God sees in infinity. We cannot judge His ways…"

"And why not? Tell me, Priest, will you indulge me just for a moment?

ASCENSION

Please, have a seat, we have time, do we not? All the time in the world..."

◊◊◊

Avila Sauerbrey saw the gaseous cloud emerge above her fellow intercessors as they continued to pray fervently under the hot Kibeho sun. She looked with concerned eyes to her companion for this pilgrimage, a holy older man called Jared. Together with a host of thousands, they prayed for the priest who was to confront the man of iniquity. It was not more than a few minutes later that she began to feel her nerves twitch all over her body.

Avila prayed for her daughter who had died suddenly as a child, but more so, she prayed for forgiveness for her own faith failing in the process, at the time, allowing herself to fall into despair. It was only after the painful death of her husband some years later that she fully rediscovered her Christian faith, even as her remaining daughter lost it.

The twitching transitioned into sharper sensations of pain as it delved deeper into her insides. Avila struggled to maintain focus, as she saw others bearing the mark of the Christian elect struggling around her, yet not leaving their positions of prayer. She would endure... the souls of many... she was sure... depended on it.

◊◊◊

"I will confess, Priest, that when I began, my motives were not so pure."

Father Daniel, seated in perhaps the most luxurious chair he had ever experienced, appeared inquisitive. "Yet, I do not sense that you are seeking absolution."

The Mystic King smiled. "Touché, my friend. It is true, I sought power, fame, the indulgence of the appetites. Yet now, what began as only a passing dream is becoming reality. Can you deny the success of Operation: Restore Spirit? Crime in the areas which we have engaged has dwindled to near nothing. People can walk anywhere in any of these cities without fear!"

"Yet at what cost, Mr. Expo?"

"Cost? It is *your* religion, in its bizarre masochistic preoccupation, that

121

demands sacrifice and glories in suffering. That is the beauty of this… it costs nothing, just a change of… *perspective*."

"Many have tried to create a utopia on Earth."

"Yes, granted, there have been many flawed approaches, but at least I am trying instead of being fatalistic—as are your followers—saying things have to get worse and waiting for some celestial superhero to jump on the scene to make everything right. And still, you Christians have the gall to call anyone who ascends to power who is not one of your own 'the antichrist.' You think I do not know that that is how you have labeled me?"

"Are you the antichrist?"

"If by antichrist you mean someone who stands opposed to the precepts of a flawed religion, I suppose by definition, I am."

◊◊◊

Peter, renewed in spirit, walked out of the giant doors of St. Peter's Basilica, where the crowds had been stirred into such a riot, that they barely noticed him. His heart sank as he saw hundreds of bodies strewn across the square… many members of the Swiss Guard, yet many more simply members of the faithful who had sought to defend him.

"It's him!" one cried out, pointing in his direction.

◊◊◊

"Drop the weapons among the throng."

"Both knives and firearms, my lord?"

Tæsír Hoc thought for a moment. He was already a bit disturbed that in not a single location had any of the throng abandoning their kneeling positions. He could see them swaying, he could see them suffering, but they stubbornly refused to move.

"Just the knives. The firearms are too quick… too easy."

◊◊◊

ASCENSION

The pain was excruciating at this point for Avila, yet it seemed that her spirit was actually growing stronger. Suddenly, blades of all forms and sizes fell from the sky. A few randomly hit their mark, fatally striking a handful of the praying crowd. Some just pierced the flesh of individuals, magnifying their pain. Yet the majority of the weapons fell around them, seemingly beckoning to them.

You can end this suffering... you have done enough...

The whispering thoughts were appealing, yet Avila would give them no quarter.

◊◊◊

"I will concede to you, Priest, there *is* a higher power—a higher intelligence. You rally around that concept with your religion, we offer Mystic Realism." He smiled as if he was about to share a great secret. "Sure, any thinking person would have to acknowledge that 'The Way' is a religion by its broadest definition. Then again, I see very few 'thinking persons' in this civilization these days. I use Mystic Realism for my own purposes. And its leaders? Especially that lovable Tæsír Hoc, use *me* for its propagation. But the point is, if there is a higher intelligence—a higher plane of existence, these religious shackles are *not* what is going to get us there."

"These 'shackles' you speak of are actually means of freedom, guiding lamps which lead towards an interior liberation that transcends our wounded natures—natures that always digress to addiction."

"No, Priest, that is not the case. These addictions you speak of are the ultimate form of freedom. It is your guilt that robs them of their liberating powers."

"You would call slavery freedom?"

"I call anything that restricts one's ability to do as they will a crime against our human spirits. But you see, Priest, we are digressing into petty squabbles of little consequence. I have discovered something that even your corrupted religion has dabbled in, yet I have perfected it. This superior intelligence—this higher plane, I have learned its language... I have harnessed its power... it is not the *word* but the *music*."

◊◊◊

"Why are they not picking up the weapons? How stupid can they be?"

"Perhaps, my lord, we need to just—"

"It was my desire for them to collapse into despair unaided. What sortilege is this? Quickly, deploy the third stage!"

"By your command, my lord."

◊◊◊

Avila felt the pulse, and it seemed as if part of her brain had caught on fire. When she thought the pain could grow no worse, she found herself suddenly *questioning* why they were even bothering with this act. It was useless, wasn't it? Who was she suffering for anyway? Was this priest feeling what she was feeling?

This life has no meaning...

She did not know where the thought found its origin, but it was not so easily dismissed.

You suffer for naught... end it... and you will be released from all of this...

Avila looked to the knife next to her and saw her hand begin to rise. The others around her were starting to moan; yet still they seemed to be fighting it. But why? She grasped the handle to the blade, began to lift it, and as she was about to bring it down upon her chest, the last vestige of hope within her called out in a commanding voice that rose above the murmuring din.

"Jesus! I trust in You!"

The blade dropped, and she was filled with a power unlike any she had experienced. Tears fell from her eyes. The physical pain was still there—perhaps even more so—but the object of her love was omnipresent. She would endure—she would, with the help of her God, be victorious.

◊◊◊

The first rock hit Peter in the back of the head, and he stumbled for a moment before righting himself and continuing. The throng, as angry as they were, seemed to be reticent to actually *touch* him. He moved forward, stepping over the dead faithful, as a second, then a third rock hit. He felt the trickle of blood come down just to the side of his cheek.

Give me strength... let every moment of my suffering be for your purposes, Lord.

◊◊◊

"I have listened to your rationalizations and justifications, Mr. Expo, but in truth, you have shared nothing new." The passion, the power in Father Daniel's voice was now clearly evident. "All of these arguments are as old as time, yet the Truth remains. As I said when I arrived, I did not come to convince you with a clever argument, yet out of love—even for you, the one who slew the young man, Phineas, whom *I* loved. I have *chosen* to love you... despite my stricken sentiments, despite wounded emotions. I choose to love, as Christ loved."

The Mystic King cocked an eyebrow beyond the coverage of his dark glasses. "Phineas, yes, the young man that you led into sin, violating the will of *my* son. Is *this* the way of your god?"

"No, it is not, and as a weak creature, I too regrettably have been a poor witness."

"Your confession is so... *touching.*"

"Yet our Sovereign, in his deepest love, is the God of forgiveness. I *have* been forgiven... for that, and many other acts against love. Your uttering it no longer has power over me. And this same forgiveness is offered to you, in love."

With that, the Mystic King shook his head in a condescending manner reflecting inner feelings of revulsion. But Father Daniel continued.

"So I ask you, I beg you, make a choice. Cease this path which you have set us—humanity—on. Do not be bound by this misguided allegiance to the eternal adversary. Hear the words of Christ, ask Him for forgiveness, His love endures forever, and His mercy is an endless ocean."

At that point, the Mystic King stood, yet Father Daniel was unable to read what was transpiring within him. "It will not work for me, Priest. What you call love is a myth. It is not within me."

"But you have a choice!"

"Then I have made my choice. And perhaps you will not be so eager to invite me into your fold when you see this."

With that, the Mystic King motioned towards the wall and twelve massive video screens emerged. The images suddenly appeared, showing thousands of the Christian Elect twisting, writhing, and contorting in agony. They were clearly attempting to maintain a prayerful posture, yet it seemed that they were about to break.

"For the love of God…" Father Daniel whispered.

"Actually, that is what I am showing you. *It does… not… exist.* Your god seems powerless to stop what is going on here, but I am giving *you* the power to change it. All you have to do is kneel before me and swear your allegiance… to *me*. I will end their suffering, and I will even dispose of the boring Tæsír Hoc, and raise you to my right hand."

"You cannot be—"

"Ananias! Do not be a fool! Your parents were gassed by religionists who hate! We could rule! Together we could transform this world in our own image! Renounce this foolish myth! Join me!"

"This cannot… I cannot…"

"End their pain! If they continue to suffer, it is because *you* continue to waffle, Ananias! Find your destiny! I offer you power beyond your wildest dreams! Not only the ability to know good and evil, but the ability to decide which is which!"

The draw of this possibility lasted only a moment. The prayers of the faithful were too great.

"No… I will not serve… *you!*"

◊◊◊

Peter was covered with a myriad of cuts and bruises upon bruises, but he had made it a good fifty meters, heading for a destination unknown. He was now stumbling over some of the thousands of dead bodies, murdered by the horde of perhaps two hundred thousand that surrounded him, yet despite their rage, they still maintained their distance. As he stepped over the last of the faithful… whom he sadly recognized as his friend and confidant, Msgr. Craig

ASCENSION

Ebright, Peter turned, his entire white cassock blood stained, and spoke.

"I forgive you, and ask the Father to forgive you. Christ is our light, our hope. May He be praised, now and forever."

Peter reached his right hand into the air, and had no sooner completed his blessing of the crowd when the shots rang out, and Pope Peter II fell lifeless to the ground.

◊◊◊

"What has happened? They have all stopped writhing. Has the weapon dissipated?"

"That is not possible, my lord."

"They are raising their hands… they are calling out praises… to *Him*!"

"What are your orders, my lord?"

"Quickly, we must silence them! Deploy the Neutron Vaporizing Device! Obliterate every cell of their being!"

"By your command, my lord."

16

"And in those final days, a portion of the Body was taken up, for there, their prayers would best serve as armaments against the impending darkness. These were the Elect, and their number was twelve times twelve thousand. The Remnant remained behind, engaged in the corporeal battle of the age."

– St. Vincent of the Sand (967-996)

i

As the sun broke in Jerusalem on the Feast of Unleavened Bread, in the time of *Neöret* 3.283, and at the command of Tæsír Hoc, Great Prophet of the Modern Age, the Neutron Vaporizing Weapon was deployed in twelve separate locations upon nearly one hundred fifty thousand members of the Christian Elect.

Though the weapon was successful in instantly vaporizing the entire throng of pilgrims, it also carried with it *unintended* consequences.

A ball of blue fire and energy formed at each epicenter, growing to a circumference of a kilometer before bursting and sending a pulsing blue wave outward at a velocity far exceeding the speed of sound. Expanding outward from the twelve epicenters, the entire globe was covered in less than ten minutes.

ASCENSION

As the pulsing blue wave swept through each citizen of the Earth, it permeated every cell of their being, and a mystical reaction within their very consciousness manifested itself; the condition of each person's tainted soul before an all-loving God was inexorably revealed to them. A tenth of the world's population perished a moment later out of profound fright, as many were unable to come to terms with the horror that had been revealed to them. Father Daniel Ananias, still standing before the Mystic King, fell to his knees, instinctively begging his God for mercy... not just for himself, but for the entire world. The Mystic King was fazed only for a moment, yet still had to steady himself.

"What... was.... *that?*"

He reached down and grabbed Father Daniel by the neck, lifting him into the air.

"I do not know what kind of sorcery this is, Priest, but as it seems the veil has been lifted, so be it, for *my* father, the Great Seraph, the Light-Bearer and Creator of Song, will defeat the Ancient of Days by crushing that which He loves most!"

The maternal presence, having been seemingly absent for so long, suddenly encompassed Father Daniel as he gasped for breath. "You have already lost..."

"And you have won *NOTHING!*"

A slight smile emerged on the face of Father Daniel Ananias.

"I do not know why you are smiling, Priest! Do you know what I am going to do to you? You will become an example for those who would oppose me. Your suffering, even amongst your thousands of martyrs, will be legendary. I promise you that..."

"That..." Father Daniel managed to get out amongst the gasps, "is one promise you will not get to keep."

"And how can you be so sure, Priest?"

"Because... I am dust... and to dust I shall return..."

And with that, before the Mystic King's eyes, a decomposition so rapid took place that the body of Father Daniel dissolved into earthen dust before Jimi T. could even react. His hand, which had maintained a firm grasp on the neck of his adversary, was left full of fine ashes.

DOMINION

ii

Nathan sat quivering, not knowing how to handle what he had just experienced. Every act he had ever engaged in during his twenty-six years on this planet had flashed before his eyes in an instant; the re-experiencing of actions that had brought harm to others—even in the remotest sense—in the company of some fully *pure* being, was agonizing. When Nathan thought things were at their worst and he could stand no more, a *presence* had suddenly become manifest, staving off the flood of self-horror.

What is this? he pondered as the emotions passed, but the memory remained ingrained in his spirit. *Such petty things... they could not have such a harmful impact... what sort of sadistic deity could hold such things against us?*

Still, Nathan was uncertain.

Who pulled the plug on that horrible experience?

He saw many of the consequences of his actions, which had a ripple effect, sometimes harming people he did not even know.

I was ignorant... I didn't know any better... and harm was not my intention. Truly, these things weren't my fault.

He continued to wrestle against the conflicting feelings within him, trying desperately to submerge the more painful ones.

Really, my parents raised me to be like this... they didn't want me to have all these moralistic hang-ups. And with everything that's happened to me, anybody would have done what I did.

But at what point was he responsible? Most certainly, given the same set of circumstances, coupled with how he had been raised and the pain he suffered, Nathan could not have been expected to do any differently, could he?

Am I really free?

But there was only silence within him.

No one... no god... could ask the impossible. If he does exist, I am just what he created me to be...

ASCENSION

iii

Twenty-four hours earlier, the world was quite different for Mikhail Ostankino. He was just preparing to exit the discothèque, reflecting on his past two years in Honduras. He arrived fully cognizant of the fact that millions had flocked to this Christian safe haven to avoid so-called religious persecution. And despite the reality that the country was now surrounded by atheistic socialist states (though truly, they were on the fast-path to swearing allegiance to The Way of Mystic Realism) Honduras seemingly maintained some sort of supernatural protection upon it.

The situation had been curious to the ambitious organized crime leader, at least superficially so, yet it was the fact that Honduras did not have—or ever desire—many of the technological advances which criminal activity so difficult in the United States. And with the millions of no-doubt weak-minded people flooding into the country, Mikhail had been sure that that he could draw many of them into a newly formed syndicate in the unsuspecting, trusting nation.

However, when the pulsing blue wave had hit him, everything was exposed, and instead of responding with a series of justifications and rationalizations, Mikhail heard his grandmother's thick Russian voice...

"Mikhail... you want to know who is responsible? Look in the mirror..."

His lungs had burned as if on fire, providing an excruciating physical pain to match that which was manifesting itself within his soul. What seemed like an eternity later, it was over, and he stood. There were a few in the discothèque weeping, but the majority of them lay on the ground, motionless, with eyes open. The expression on their faces was as much anger as it was fear.

Then, without a second thought, Mikhail heeded his grandmother's command, as he looked at himself in the mirror on the opposite side of the bar counter. The still lit cigarette fell from his hands.

And that had led him here. On the edge of the recently expanded town of Comayagua, he stood before a door to a Franciscan Friary which read, *"Convento de San Serafin."*

He had not bared his soul to a priest in almost four decades.

"No time better than the present, Mikhail... let's do this."

He knocked on the door, and nothing would ever again be the same.

DOMINION

iv

"People of Israel, chosen people of One True God! Hear me, *Adonai* has spoken, and He desires that you come to know Him through His Son, who became flesh in the form of Jesus of Nazareth. He is the Christ prophesied of old. Your forefathers were misled, a proud yet fallen people. They put this man, Jesus, to death, but He is risen! Repent, and hear the good news!"

Enoch and Elijah moved through the streets of Israel; there were millions of Jewish souls to attend to. Each of the Witnesses preached aloud in multiple venues, speaking of the imminent return of the Messiah. Many, following the "incident" only days before, were willing to permit this message to speak to their hearts and were baptized. Others, however, held out, tenaciously grasping the faith of their forefathers. Yet the largest group seemed shaken yet unmoved; something had happened, but they heard that the Mystic King would be making a statement shortly, explaining this strange phenomenon, returning their society to the 'normalcy' that the majority of its inhabitants craved.

They had learned that most of Europe had—essentially overnight— reclaimed its Christian roots... the result of tens of thousands of primarily Russian missionaries making the soil fertile for the strange self-awareness that had been impressed on the population. Rumors abounded of great assemblies of "reverted" Christian faithful throughout Africa, East Asia, and even the United States.

These were strange days, all agreed. Much excitement—some optimistic, some anxious. Though it would soon pass, most would say...

Nothing endures forever...

v

"Citizens of the world, I realize that the incident that took place last week at the Hebrew Feast of Unleavened Bread has caused great confusion and emotional distress to you all. We have assembled the greatest minds in the world to investigate the source of this strange manifestation, which some—and I fear many—have tried to frame as being Divine in origin."

Jimi T. spoke with authority to the itching ears of the masses, utilizing every channel and every frequency known to humanity. There had been a brief disruption in his plan, but its impact was already beginning to fade.

"Do not underestimate the capacity of the human mind to dismiss that which is uncomfortable," the Mystic King had told the somewhat crestfallen Tæsír Hoc, who was now, once again, called to stand at his side.

"We have learned that this was the greatest of deceptions, initiated with diabolical intentions by the *Dishalåk*. Through a series of chemical compounds activated by a magnetic pulse, these deceivers were able to draw on the vestiges of old myths which still exist in the more primal regions of each of our minds... creating sensations of guilt and fear in an attempt to close off our access to the *Kôles*. Sadly, many true believers perished, as the experience of being completely separated from the *Kôles* is one that is more than man can bear. But as is also evident, those who had spent more of their past energies in these false religions were the most susceptible, and the most readily fooled by this ploy.

"In order to restore order, we have deployed seven million troops of the Global Communion Peacekeeping Force around the world, as well as twelve thousand newly ordained *Rætôi*, so I would encourage calm... peace will be restored, despite the twisted desires of the *Dishalåk*.

"Be vigilant, my brothers and sisters, for they are among us. Do not heed their words. We are on the brink of a great transformation; do not let the fears of old be a barrier to our collective liberation..."

17

The Signs of the Times ح
<<n 4.272>>

MECCA - The Islamic religion officially came to a close yesterday, with last month's decree issued by Caliph Ali Bakr reaching its effective date of consummation.

"We have done our part, we have fulfilled our purpose," the undisputed 12th Imam shared at the central shrine of the Muslim people. "While for a season, Islam laid the foundation, The Way of Mystic Realism is the eternal answer, and we must all now shed that which is not of the *Kôles* and accept our rightful place of leadership in the coming age that is upon us."

The response of the Muslim people has been near immediate. In the past four weeks, a period prescribed by the Imam, nearly a billion have accepted their liberation, receiving The Seal of Mystic Realism. Sadly, though not surprisingly, since the 'Great Deception' a year ago, nearly five hundred million former Muslims have fallen under the spell of the *Ďishalák*, and now identify themselves as Christian.

An independent study has confirmed that the past year's swell of those identifying themselves as Christian has leveled off in nearly all nations and is now beginning a rapid decline in most. As of this week, it is estimated that 57% of the world population is now fully aligned with The Way of Mystic Realism. Christianity has peaked at 40%.

ASCENSION

        With the joint statement issued
three months ago by leaders of the
Buddhist, Hindu, and related eastern
religions, definitively expressing that
there are no doctrinal contradictions
between their belief systems and those
of The Way, the once convoluted
divisions among existential approaches
are no more; the forces of truth and
liberation are now fully united against
the opposing forces of deception and
enslavement.

        As the world moves towards the
impending close of the Jewish allegory
with the dedication of the Third Temple,
it is unclear how many will still be
claiming this religious affiliation at
that time. While roughly a third still
cling to the ways of Judaism, the same
number have already professed allegiance
to The Way, following Rabbi Solomon
Abram's disclosure of the Mystic King's
Jewish roots, being descended of the
Tribe of Dan. Most have recognized this
as a clear indicator of Jimi T. Expo's
identity as the promised Messiah.

        Though the deceptive activities
of the *Dishalåk* have had some success in
luring as many as six million Jews from
the truth, this fad is considered to be
temporary. It is anticipated that all
will come under the fold at the Temple's
impending dedication.

DOMINION

i

In the time of *Neöret* 4.276, the Mystic King stood on the steps of St. Peter's Basilica, looking out over the millions of followers who filled Saint Peter's Square. He looked down to Caleb, who beamed up to him from his right side. He glanced briefly to his left, where Tæsír Hoc, his nearly loyal and steadfast Prophet stood.

"Tell them, Abba!" Caleb prodded excitedly. He had now reached the age of eight, but had still not mastered the concept of patience.

"Very well, my son," Jimi T. responded, then stepped forward to speak to the throng.

"It has been one year, ample time for the *Cortät* to reclaim their place of worship."

Many nods and affirmative calls swept through the crowd.

"Perhaps many have recognized the sheer vanity of their movement. Though acknowledging that their number has briefly peaked since the Great Deception, they are a beast without a head. In time, that will change... I sense this with assurance. The time is rapidly approaching when those *Cortät* who call themselves Christian will be given one final opportunity to embrace their liberation."

Some random cheers emerged from the masses.

"Though I must admit, the *Cortät* were right about one thing. This *is* a holy place. The Spirit's presence here is strong, and I can see how even the earliest Christians misinterpreted that presence to be that of their mythological god. But it is because of the strong presence of the Spirit that I hereby claim this site for The Way of Mystic Realism and announce the relocation of the Global Communion to this dwelling of great mysticism."

A roar shot through the crowd, and Caleb instinctively hugged the man who had brought this all about.

And the Mystic king called out, "If the Spirit is with us, then who can be against?"

ASCENSION

ii

Sawlus finished keying in the last few words of her transmission as the van she was in screeched around the corner. She knocked on the floor twice, and the older woman in the passenger seat looked back. Sawlus lifted both hands up in a questioning gesture.

Annie D. looked to the readout on the electrical device she was holding, then responded, "Aye, they're still trackin' our signal, but we have little choice. Send the transmission, and we'll be trustin' the good Lord on this one... again!"

Sawlus nodded and typed in her closeout to the transmission;

> Continue to be strong, my Christian brothers and sisters, for we are in the latter days, as prophesied. Hold strong to your beliefs on this celebration of the Resurrection of our Lord, and know that what is must come to pass in order to glorify the Father. In Christ's name we pray...
>
> *– The Convert*

She pressed the button marked "Voice Box Simulator" then followed it with "Send". Sawlus knew they would only actually be online for an instant, while the coded and condensed transmission was sent to the network's lone satellite. It would then be transmitted back both in text and voice in real-time across the world.

It had been difficult, this past year, without Father Daniel directing their activities and providing spiritual support. Before his departure for what was to be his final assignment, he had requested that the woman, Annie D., take up his mantle in leading what remained of their small team. Sawlus was grateful that both Annie and Bud continued to respect the request of the priest, not pushing her for any additional information as to her identity or calling. Truly, Sawlus felt as if even she could not provide sufficient answers at this point.

The van made another quick turn before accelerating down a back street. From the front seat, Annie undid her belt and moved to the back of the van with Sawlus.

"Looks like we got another one off, darlin'... without a hitch!" she exclaimed, providing Sawlus with a gentle smile. Sawlus had found herself growing increasingly fond of that Irish smile, Annie's maternal nurturance, and unwavering faith.

Her task completed, Sawlus put down the transmitter and slumped down in the back corner of the van, rubbing her eye with the butt of her hand and sighing.

"You've been dreamin' of him again, haven't you?" Annie D. inquired.

Sawlus nodded solemnly.

"You've got to have faith, pet! When it all boils down to it, that's all we've got."

Sawlus looked up at Annie with a disinterested expression. Annie D. cocked her head and provided a smile of understanding.

"I see what your thinkin', pet. Your thinkin', 'what does this old, well-to-do Irish woman know about sufferin'?' Am I right?"

Sawlus did not alter her gaze, but shrugged.

"Aye, I thought as much. Well, let me tell you, luv, we've known each other for a good eighteen months now. Father had seen fit to keep your identity hidden, and I'm respectin' him for it. Though still, I've gotten to know a few of your old demons, so I s'pose it's high time I tell you a few of mine."

Sawlus smiled to herself. There were only four people in the Christian Remnant who knew her previous identity, and now two were dead, with the other two preaching throughout Israel and various other regions of the world. For safety's sake, she had managed to keep this identity to herself, only identifying herself as "The Convert." But in reflecting on Annie D.'s question, Sawlus' clear response was "no"; there was no possibility such an optimistic, well-to-do woman like Annie D. could know the first thing about true suffering.

"I grew up in Belfast in the midst of much turmoil. My parents, God bless them, shunned the 'family business', the Irish Republican Militia, believing there was a better way. Despite their innocence, they were eventually driven out of their homeland after my uncle ordered the murder of a couple whose only crime was bein' related to Great Britain's prime minister."

Sawlus' eyes widened.

"Ach, I suppose I have gotten ahead of myself, there though," Annie D. apologized. "I had meself already left Ireland at the time. I married a Ruskie, I did; and not exactly the most honest kind, I might add. And in me seventy-two years, I've buried him, all three of me children, and me only two grandchildren." She sighed deeply, as her eyes began to fill. "Truth is, though, I made me bed, I made me choices… and now I'm all alone."

Sawlus looked at Annie D. sympathetically, feeling guilty over her own presumptuousness.

"But, darlin'," Annie D. continued in a concluding tone, "if there is one thing I still got, it's faith, and I plan on dyin' with that same faith. One way or another, you'll be gettin' your son back, of that I'm certain. I've prayed for him, and claimed him for the Lord. Remember, we've got the Almighty on our side—we won't be losin' this war."

With that, Sawlus nodded sadly. It was true, they did have the Almighty on their side, but that did not change the fact that all had not proceeded as it seemed the Almighty had planned. Though she loved her Lord, and would never again forsake Him, Sawlus could not help but wonder if perhaps He had taken His adversary too lightly over all those eons, and now *His Infernal Majesty* was back with a plan. Was there a supernatural law that, in the end, good must *always* triumph over evil? Or perhaps, was prophecy no more than one entity's plan for the future as He would *like* to see it?

"Take heart, luv. Though the times are dark, it's a battle worth fightin'."

iii

Nathan sat nervously in the third row of media personnel assembled for this announcement. His lame disguise, a baseball cap covering most of his buzz cut and bleached hair, along with a pair of glasses, seemed to be doing the trick, but the reality was, he had pretty much become yesterday's news.

Carl Woodward patted him on the back clandestinely, in a supportive fashion, as he moved up to the podium, prepared to announce the release of *The Phoenix – Risen Son*. The free-verse prose of Jonathan's had been released immediately after the so-called "Great Deception", but this was truly the big day, as far as Nathan was concerned.

As Carl began to speak, a hand rested on Nathan's shoulder. "Hey, old buddy."

Nathan turned his head quickly to lay his eyes on none other than Siro Scribner. He jumped with a start. "Yeah, that's right, like seeing a ghost. It's been a while… what, two years? You've caused quite a stir, my friend, and you are about to do some more."

Siro spoke with a whisper, but still a bit too loud for Nathan's comfort. Yet even so, it seemed like all eyes and ears were currently locked on Carl Woodward.

Nathan feigned ignorance. "What are you talking about?"

Siro frowned. "Come on, Nathaniel. You think I couldn't figure out who released those old poems of Jonathan Storm's? And really, your old band? Don't you remember it was *me* that cracked that murder-corruption case following the accident that killed your friend?"

"My name is not associated in any way with the *e*Album. Nobody has to know I had anything to do with it. I owe it to Jes— er, Jonathan."

Siro paused and shook his head, contemplating his next comment carefully.

"Jimi T. knows."

Nathan's head jerked around. "What do you mean? What does he know?"

"You think he doesn't remember Jonathan or *The Phoenix*? Are you more stupid than you look, my friend? You guys were his last line of competition for the big time." He paused for a moment, then glanced up at Woodward. "And hooking up with this snake-oil salesman... really, Nathaniel. The guy used to work for me. He's bad news."

Nathan pondered the prospect momentarily and wondered how he could have let that slip by. "This was not against Jimi T. or anyone else. It is strictly a tribute to an old friend."

"Under a Christian label? Yeah, they claim otherwise, but this is reality. What the hell has gotten into you, Nathaniel? Are you blind to what's going on in the world? We are on the verge of total peace, in our families, neighborhoods, and nations, and it's all because of Jimi T. and The Way. And it may never have been needed if it weren't for the *Cortät* whom you now associate with. He gave you the chance of a lifetime, and you're throwing it all back in his face."

"You make it sound like I'm intentionally trying to ruin him!" Nathan defended. "In actuality, this has nothing to do with him."

"Doesn't it, Nathaniel? Well that's not how it seems from here. I'm going to level with you, buddy. Jimi T. sent me here to retrieve you."

"*What?*"

Siro nodded. "That's right. So that he can instill some sense back in you. Each member of *Çön Razón* made a commitment to end their creative careers once the band had been dissolved, and you broke that promise."

Nathan turned his head to look back up at Carl, who was now raising his hands, accepting the audience's applause. He turned back to Siro with a more somber, uncomfortable tone.

"So did… did it happen to you too?"

Siro was perplexed. "What the hell are you talking about?"

"The illumination. You know. seeing your own soul?"

Siro was clearly frustrated at this point, yet the question posed obviously opened a sense of insecurity within him. "Listen, Nathaniel, that was a trick, a manipulation. Didn't you listen to anything Jimi T. said? Are you that tied up with these *Cortäf*?"

"Absolutely not. I'm not a Christian, and I never have been. But Jonathan was. I have no doubt this was what he would have wanted, no matter how misguided."

"Then you better hope that nothing comes of this."

Nathan nodded, then looking back to the front, spoke resolutely. "Listen, Siro, I need a favor. Don't tell Jimi T. that you saw me here."

Siro looked as if he had been stabbed in the chest. "Are you out of—?"

"Just for now," Nathan interrupted. "Just until I can clear a few more things in my mind, and then I promise, I'll go to Jimi T. and sort this all out."

"I can't—"

"You have to, Siro. I've been your friend for years, and I'm asking you to be one now. Unless you plan on bringing me in by force, let me go. I will return, maybe as the prodigal son, to pay the piper."

18

"Music has a power of forming the character,
and should therefore be introduced into the
education of the young."

- Aristotle

i

Caleb and the boy called Abram cruised their solar-bikes into the driveway of the last house on Emmaus Drive. Caleb was especially ecstatic this day, as he had just received his audio implants in his inner earlobe. He would now be able to listen—via satellite—to *Çön Razón*, as well as other emerging bands in the *Hôlmüs* genre, 24/7. In its smart technology, the implant could modify the volume based on its ability to detect a conversation. What was even cooler—at least in Caleb's eyes—was that any form of formal education would now be unnecessary. The implant provided for all academic subjects, which were fused with the music in a manner which transmitted information directly to the applicable part of the brain… no attention necessary.

The two boys disembarked, and Caleb drew back his sleeve to reveal his new *iBerry II* strapped to his wrist. He tapped its screen a few times, looked up at the house address, and then back down to his virtual pad.

"This is the place," he stated calmly.

"I thought it would be bigger," Abram responded.

Caleb moved to the front door, and Abram, being a year his junior, followed.

Caleb rang the door chime, and then waited patiently. A voice came out across the intercom.

"Yes?"

"Mr. Woodward?" Caleb inquired.

"Can you do me the favor of identifying who is asking?" the voice requested.

Caleb closed his eyes and opened his mind to the Spirit of the *Kôles*. His eyes opened.

"We have been sent by Father Liam Ebright. We have news on the whereabouts of Jonathan Storm."

The intercom cut off and suddenly the front door opened. A man stepped forward, then immediately stopped.

"What? Who are you?" he demanded. "You're with the *Neo Mystè*. If you please, I'm not interested in whatever you are selling. Please go. Good day."

Carl Woodward, having developed a more than slight sense of paranoia following a few threats relating to the release of Jonathan Storm's material, attempted to close the door quickly but found that it would not budge.

"Why are you so set, Mr. Woodward, on ruining the happiness of billions?"

Woodward continued to try to shake the door free. "Happiness? You are very young and very misled, boy. Happiness comes from loving the Lord and one's fellow man, not from worshiping what feels good or exciting for the moment. Confound this door!"

"Here, let me help," Caleb offered and reached his hand up to the door. It immediately broke free.

Woodward looked perplexed. "Well, thank you. I don't know what quite got into this." He looked back to Caleb. "Now you two go run along. It's getting late, and I'm sure your mothers are worried about you."

"I don't have a mother."

Woodward was caught off-guard as he felt a sudden twinge of sadness seep into his consciousness. His anxiety-turned-anger dissipated. "Well, your father then, run along."

"I have to leave you with a gift!" Caleb spurted.

Woodward shook his head. "No, thank you, son. Now please, have a good—"

But Caleb burst into tears. "My f-father, he'll beat me if I don't get rid of this last gift! He *knows* when I screw up, he always knows!"

Woodward looked down upon Caleb, feeling a wave of pity for the poor misguided child. He looked to the other boy, who also reflected a melancholic nature. Sure the kid was probably manipulating him, but it couldn't hurt just to humor him… especially if it would get him off his front doorstep more quickly.

Woodward smiled somewhat impatiently. "Okay, kid, I'll take the gift, and then you just head on home, right?"

Caleb smiled through his tears. "Okay!"

Caleb had Abram turn around, and he reached into his backpack. He pulled out a crystal with a thin leather strap that would allow it to be worn around the neck.

"It's a drawing crystal," he said.

Woodward took the crystal from Caleb somewhat absently. "Okay, thank you, young man, now you run along."

"Okay, thanks, mister!"

Carl Woodward walked back into his kitchen, feeling a fleeting sense of relief. He held the crystal up to the light, and had to admit a slight experience of aesthetic appreciation for it. He smiled, shook his head, and then tossed it into his incinerator.

He walked over to his refrigerator and opened the door…

There, wrapped around the top of his milk carton, was a perfect duplicate of the crystal.

Not only that, there was a second crystal lying in the butter tray.

"What the…?"

He immediately became anxious. He grabbed the two crystals, praying to himself that the boys had a third companion who had planted these two, then threw them into the incinerator.

Woodward stepped into his dining room, and gasped as he saw four crystals dangling from his overhead light.

"Lord help me," he whispered as he reached furiously for the four, only to notice a fifth and a sixth in his foyer.

He continued to destroy the crystals, some in his garbage disposal, more in the incinerator, and he even began smashing them with a hammer.

ASCENSION

After the destruction of several hundred crystals, in vain he sprinted up to his bedroom and locked the door.

He closed his eyes, his back against the door, and breathed heavily.

"You forgot this one, mister!"

Woodward opened his eyes in horror and saw the boy from the *Neə Mĭ̦stè* standing at the other end of his room, dangling the crystal in his hand.

Woodward attempted to call out as he watched the crystal disappear from the boy's hand, but for some reason, he could not. He felt a tightness around his neck, and to his terror realized that the crystal was wrapped around his throat, and the band was tightening more and more.

He let out a brief gurgle as he fell to his knees, trying to grasp the straps. A blood red glow began to emanate from the crystal. Woodward fell into a crawl and desperately moved across the room …

His last motion on this Earth was the extension of his right arm, reaching for the crucifix situated above his bed.

ii

Tæsír Hoc stood before the masses on the bank of the River Jordan. An estimated thirteen million followers had assembled here, guided to this place only by the Spirit of the *Kôles*.

"My brothers and sisters," he began. "May the *Kôles* be within you."

"AND WITH YOUR SPIRIT!" the masses responded with the sound of thunder.

Tæsír Hoc smiled widely, closed his eyes, and inhaled deeply. "I bring to you a message from our Mystic King, a message only for the most faithful to the *Kôles*. Are there those of you among us here today worthy of the Word?"

"WE ARE WORTHY, TEACHER," they responded. "SAY THE WORD, THAT WE MAY BE ENLIGHTENED."

The Prophet nodded and proceeded with his message. "We are quickly approaching the end day, and drastic times require drastic measures. We feel that the *Cortät* have been given ample opportunity to convert, yet we must take this invitation one step further. For our King still sees them as our lost brothers and sisters, so we must help them if there is but one speck of the Spirit left within them.

"From this day forth, we will seek out the misled and provide for them locations, Purification Centers if you will, for their souls to be more assertively sought after. This is your calling, my brothers and sisters, and it is the will of our Sovereign and King. Will you stand with us in our quest to provide our great gift to even the lowliest of *Cortät*?"

"WE WILL!" they responded, and continued to shout until the earth shook.

With that, Tæsír Hoc turned as his assistant approached him with his cloak. Underneath the roar of the crowd, the Prophet spoke.

"As far as I'm concerned," he muttered between gritted teeth, "all these *Cortät* hold-outs can choke on their own vomit. Jimi T. has been far too lenient with the scourge. They are an infection which must be obliterated."

"It's a step in the right direction, isn't it?" the assistant responded as he placed the cloak across the Prophet's shoulders and the two moved towards his private helicopter.

"Yes, and what's more, Terrence, it has been bestowed upon me to oversee the camps as I see fit."

They hopped into the helicopter, and the pilot called back, "To the Jerusalem airport, as planned, Mr. Aborn?"

"Yes, and let's move it!" Terrence responded.

He looked back to Tæsír Hoc, who maintained a fiendish grin on his face. "Our Sovereign follows the line of the shepherd who leaves the flock of ninety-nine to find the one lamb who has gone astray." He licked his lips and smiled even wider.

"But as far as I'm concerned, the one be damned! Let us prepare the ninety-nine for slaughter, as it is high time for a feast!"

iii

Sawlus picked up the large manila envelope with some apprehension. Bud Petrall had returned to her one-time secret residence in Florham Park, New Jersey, and found it burned to the ground. He shared that most likely those responsible had first scoured the place for anything that could have provided a clue to her disappearance, then set it ablaze afterwards. The envelope had somehow survived the fire, and when she saw Caleb's name scribbled upon it, she found her heart filled with gratitude. These were his favorite drawings, which he had hidden away somewhere in the basement.

"For a rainy day," he had said.

She pulled out a small stack of drawings and began to look through them as her eyes filled with tears of joy as well as remorse. As she began to cling to what little she had left of her son, Annie D. knocked at the door.

"Please excuse an old woman for intrudin'." Annie D. spoke apologetically. "Bud told me what he'd recovered. A blessin', it is… and hopefully one that will keep your spirits up."

Sawlus nodded as she looked back to the papers and continued to move through them.

"I've received word that a priest will be comin' our way in the next few weeks. It seems all the seminarians and deacons are gone, save a few. We thought the government leavin' the deacons was an act of mercy, but it's clear… it was only a ruse to keep our guard down, and then draw us out."

Sawlus looked up again, only half-hearing what Annie was saying as the emotions and memories seemed to wipe her attention span clean.

Annie readily sized up the situation. "Forgive me, pet. We can talk later. I'll leave ya with yer thoughts for now."

Sawlus provided a grateful acknowledgment as she flipped to the next drawing. Annie was already turning herself when it caught her eye. "Good Lord, would you look at that? That can't be one of Caleb's, luv, could it?"

Sawlus gasped herself as she looked at the perfectly drawn sketch of a man's face, yet with a name below clearly scribbled in the writing of a near four-year-old.

Simon

DOMINION

iv

Nathan walked along the Waterside district of Norfolk, Virginia, gazing across the Elizabeth River on a clear August night. He had much to ponder at this point, as he walked, guitar strapped to his back, looking for a quiet bench to sit at and play.

Back in April, after thinking it through and discussing the matter with Carl Woodward, Nathan had made a single transfer of funds from his personal account into that of Woodward's *The Alternative* publishing corporation, the same day of the announcement of the release of Jonathan's music. He was conservative, keeping it under a million *Ameros*, but he also took the liberty, as much as for a decoy as anything else, of making other transfers of the same amount to every name of any old friend or acquaintance he could recall.

Merry Christmas in April, friends!

It had barely put a dent in his account. In turn, Woodward hired a publicity agency for the promotion of Jonathan Storm's music and poetry. He far overpaid the group, with the understanding that they would also rent a townhouse and keep a recurring order of groceries going there weekly. Just what Nathan needed to maintain his low profile, at least until... until...

He did not really know at this point. The "event" had taken place sixteen months ago, which Nathan still felt he was processing. The release of poetry was the next week, and the music a year later. And now it had been nearly four months since the announcing press conference, and the response was... nothing?

Nathan had learned earlier that week that Carl had died of an apparent brain aneurysm. *The Alternative* had been shut down, though Nathan knew that Woodward had gotten all of the electronic media to a multitude of distributors before any with bad feelings towards the music could get to it.

So what do I do now?

He stopped at the streetlight, walked up to the edge of the sidewalk, and looked down onto his reflection in the water.

"Don't jump, buddy."

Nathan was so startled that he almost *did* fall in. He wheeled around to see his old friend, Siro, as well as another familiar face, Kako Edgar. Though Kako looked a lot different than before. In an instant, Nathan recalled the loss of his *Þreha* in a car accident a couple years back. It didn't look like time had healed any wounds.

"Hey, Siro," Nathan tried to sound casual. "Hey, Kako. Man, don't you look like shit."

A flash of anger swept across Kako's eyes. "Yeah? Well, I'll be feeling a lot better in a few minutes after I kick your ass." And with that, Kako stepped forward and grabbed Nathan by the collar.

"Dude! Dude! Chill out! I bruise easy."

Siro put a hand on Kako's shoulder. "Easy, Kako, I'm sure Nathaniel's ready to come with us of his own free will."

But Nathan, despite his predicament, shook his head rapidly. "Oh no... no way. I'm just starting to get a grip on things. I haven't had any nutty dreams in weeks. I'm out, guys, I'm telling you... I'm out!"

"The only thing you're out of," Kako spoke through gritted teeth as he reached into his pocket, "is luck."

Kako pulled the stun-stick from his pocket and pressed it to Nathan's stomach. Nathan screamed for only an instant, but his body unexpectedly produced a brief glow, then a flash, and he was suddenly...

"What happened?" Siro gasped, terrified. "Where did he go?"

Kako himself was in utter bewilderment. "I don't... I don't know... it's never done that before."

"Oh shit!" Siro was bordering on hysteria as a million implications regarding what just happened shot through his head. "You vaporized him! You stupid fuck! He's gone!"

Nathan had felt the shock, and had then experienced the sensation of falling backwards. As he prepared to hit the water, he found himself lying on solid ground. *Grassy* ground.

"What the—?"

He turned, and once again saw the familiar tree on the grassy knoll. There at the foot of the tree, right where he had left him, was a still distraught Ralph Tobit.

"Damn! I was doing so well!"

Nathan stood up, and found that his guitar still remained on his back, gratefully intact, having made the trip with him. Not knowing what else to do at this juncture but go along with the vision, he proceeded towards Ralph, who seemed unprepared for his new guest and jumped with a start.

"What are you doing?" he cried. "I thought I asked you to leave me."

"Well, you did," Nathan said apologetically, "and, I did. But that was a few years ago."

"Years?" Ralph was clearly confused. "You stepped away not more than a moment ago."

Nathan was speechless. "I-I'm sorry. I don't understand what all this is… or what's happening. I'm clearly a pawn in all of this."

Ralph looked up at Nathan, his eyes squinting in an attempt to focus on the guitar. "What is that you have there?" he inquired. "It has a… a certain *familiarity* about it."

Nathan frowned. "It's… ahh… called a guitar." Then with his notable sarcasm, he added, "And what planet did you come from?"

Ralph appeared puzzled by the statement, but was not dissuaded. "I believe it is a medium for drawing out music, is it not?"

Nathan cocked his head curiously. "Ahh, well, actually, it makes the music."

Ralph suddenly laughed, only briefly, but was clearly amused by the statement. "No, music is not created by an object. Its genesis is in the soul. Life comes from life. These mediums only give it a voice."

At this point, Nathan was truly intrigued. "I've never thought of it that way."

This clearly did not make sense to Ralph. "Do you not know its language?"

"Its language?"

It was clear that Ralph was losing patience. "Go ahead, take the guitar… draw out the music… give it its voice."

Nathan shrugged and pulled the guitar out in front of him. Without giving it much thought, he began to pluck an arpeggio from a song he and Jimi T. had written.

Suddenly, Ralph screamed out in horrible agony, grabbing his ears. The disintegrating 'blink' suddenly manifested itself again, as if all of his cells were being drawn apart.

Nathan stopped immediately, and Ralph's body, momentarily having taken on a transparent nature, drew back together. He breathed a sigh of relief.

"You do not know... you do not know the language of the Sovereign."

Nathan was almost paralyzed by what he had just done. "I-I am sorry. I don't know what..."

"You must try again. I sense the absence that is present in your spirit. But that is not all that is there. Give a voice to that which defies the absence."

Nathan was hesitant to try again.

"You must," Ralph commanded.

Nathan thought for another moment then suddenly remembered an old tune; one he had never really heard in its fullness, but the one Jonathan had begun to play that fateful night on the harpsichord. He closed his eyes momentarily, heard the song in his spirit, and then began to pluck the strings.

"Yes..." Ralph breathed, his voice sounding as one who had just in a cool drink. "Yes... that is it... that is the language of the Sovereign."

Nathan stopped, not having heard more than a few bars of the song himself. Ralph's eyes, which had briefly closed for the moment, opened.

"It is unfinished... words have been left unsaid, yes?"

Nathan nodded, suddenly struck with a wave of sadness. "Yes, I suppose so."

A moment passed, and Nathan posed the question that had been on his mind. "I need help, Ralph. I need to make sense of all of this. But now, you seem to be more lost than I."

"I do not know this 'Ralph'."

"I know... somehow you've forgotten. But where I come from—"

"Where do you come from?"

"I-I don't know. The real world. But there, your name is Ralph. You help people... like a protector... a guardian."

Ralph attempted to scour his memory. "I do not recall such a place."

Nathan thought for a moment, then a concept suddenly struck him.

"Wait a minute! Maybe you're just like me! Maybe you're dreaming this as well, only somehow, you're having a hard time coming out of the dream."

Ralph looked at Nathan without comprehension, but this did not dissuade Nathan. He continued.

"Then what I have to do... I have to find you. In my world. Maybe you're in a coma or something. I'll find you, and I'll... I'll draw you out." His mind flashed back to Jonathan, years ago lying on his bed. "I've done it before."

And with that, Nathan suddenly felt himself being propelled backwards to that plane of existence he so desired to escape, yet so desired to embrace.

"...I've done it before."

19

i

"You have heard of the earthquake in Arabia, my lord?"

Jimi T. nodded. "Yes, I sensed its occurrence."

The Mystic King leaned back in his chair, admiring his Vatican office acquired a little more than a year before. He reflected with relish on the many Popes who had occupied this place before him. The view of Saint Peter's Square was definitely one to die for.

"Well," General Orieton continued, a bit hesitant because of the perceived lack of interest on Jimi T.'s part. "It seems that there was more to this whole situation now."

Jimi T. looked curiously at him and sat up, hands folded on the table. "Speak."

Orieton hesitated for a moment before proceeding. "Well, it appears there were several *million* troops stationed in that area at the time."

"Arabian troops?" Jimi T. inquired.

"Yes, my lord, along with a mass of military artillery and equipment."

Jimi T. thought for a moment, then stood and walked over to his world map, which covered the entire south wall of his office.

"And where exactly were these troops stationed?"

"Nineveh, my lord, at the epicenter of the quake. It seems they had descended from northern Turkey, and had occupied Kurdistan."

Jimi T. looked momentarily perplexed. "How could this possibly happen without that big-mouthed King not calling down fire from every end of the Earth? His revulsion towards anything that carries an Islamic scent is well known."

Orieton nodded. "I can only assume he was somehow... *persuaded*, my lord, to permit these troops to hide there."

The Mystic King mulled the idea for the moment. "It would seem, not surprisingly so, that the *Cortät* King is an owned man." He then reflected a bit more, as he reached his hand up and rubbed his chin. The enigmatic slight grin emerged from his face.

"They were mobilizing to invade Israel, and defy my decree."

"My lord?"

But Jimi T. was already several steps beyond explaining what he now knew to be the truth to Orieton. He walked right up to his general and spoke.

"I am going to say this only once, so listen closely. An international embargo is to be instated on the Arabian Empire effective immediately, and an emergency session of the G.C. must be arranged within seven days. The Caliph must answer to these charges, which I am bringing before the Council."

"Yes, my lord."

"I will be calling for the mobilization of twenty million troops of the G.C. Peacekeeping Force to surround the Israeli borders. And finally..."

"Yes, my lord?"

"I want an immediate, covert investigation initiated into any connection that the Soviet Union or Chinese Empire may have with this situation."

ii

"He knows! I have been summoned!"

Luther had never seen Anaxagoras so anxious in all the time he had known him. He found the display mildly amusing.

"Do not be afraid, Anaxagoras. The Anointed needs the Caliph Ali Bakr for at least one more task… as he does the good Rabbi."

"I do not believe that is so. I have already disassembled Islam according to plan. Really, it was never my intent to actually confront him.. only to serve as a reminder that he needs us to bring the fullness of the Master's plan into fruition."

"And to perhaps put a little fly in his ointment?"

Anaxagoras relaxed slightly. "Well, yes, I did want to prevent this misguided desire to establish order from becoming a reality. I agree with your previous sentiments, Luther, that such a thing could lead the masses into *hope*.. placing us on enemy territory."

"I am surprised you were able to still find three million Jew-hating Muslims, Anaxagoras."

"I had little choice. Those who I knew would not believe the 'Islam is completed' line—I informed their leaders that this was just a deception to get Israel to lower its guard. I had three hundred Soviets training and leading them. These troops would ultimately be slaughtered, I was sure, but not before dealing an incredible blow against the Jews."

"…and our apparently Jew-loving Mystic King?"

Anaxagoras looked steadily back at Luther, feeling every bit his near twelve hundred years. Luther knew his situation was truly dire but was not about to let on. He continued.

"I myself do not understand what has happened to our *Anointed*… though his actions with the *Cortät*—specifically those who referred to themselves as the Christian Elect—show me that he is not completely lost."

"What are we to do?"

Luther pondered this thought momentarily before speaking. "He has many enemies other than us. For now, we just draw our protection back enough so that he may feel the heat. You can trust me; he will get the picture very soon. But the Council must be united in this, lest we allow him to divide us and destroy us out of his own need for control. I will speak to them. Their hearts are the Master's, and any previous reservations will certainly have abated by now."

DOMINION

iii

"So, you're the music man Morris told me about?"

"Yes, sir. Really, just looking for a place to play for a few days."

The owner of Catacomb Tavern eyed Nathan suspiciously as he absently chewed the end of his pipe. "Morris tells me I won't regret having you... says you're as good as they come, and that you aren't playing that manipulative crap that passes for music these days."

Nathan could not help but chuckle. "No, sir, mostly original stuff that I think would be to your liking, some covers from an old friend, along with a few oldies."

In many ways, Nathan was having the time of his life. He had returned from his final vision of Ralph in pretty much the same location where he had had his scuffle with Kako and Siro, but it did not take long for him to realize he had again lost time. This time, it was nearly six months.

No big deal... I'm rolling with the punches now.

He did not wait around for long to embark on his new mission—finding Ralph, the mysterious paramedic, who he was sure was probably either laying in a coma somewhere or wandering the streets in some amnesia-like state. Nathan was not even certain that this enigmatic man could help him put together all the pieces of this world, and enlighten Nathan as to his part in it. He was only certain that he needed to find him.

"I think that'll work just fine, son. The folk around here are simple... by choice. That's why we kept this town as it is. This so-called 'progress', at least how we see it, is nothing more than old vices with newer packaging."

Nathan nodded. There was something about the simplicity of these retro-towns that he found attractive, though he was pretty certain it was not for him. No doubt, these were closet-Christians.

"Yes, sir. Did Morris tell you? I'm only looking for room and board for a week or so in exchange for playing. Then a ride to the next town, and if you're pleased, a reference."

The man nodded, drawing his pipe to his lips for another puff. "Agreed. In reality, that's probably all we have to offer."

That's how it had been for the past four months, hitting nearly two-dozen retro-towns as he slowly made his way across the country. He knew these anti-progress—and now anti-government—towns would be his safest bet in keeping a low profile as he set out upon this quest. They could keep a secret well, and were not prone to asking probing questions. What he had *not* expected was what he was soon to discover in each one of these localities.

"There is one other thing," Nathan started in as he pulled a sketched picture from his guitar case. In the first retro-town he played at, a place called Buckingham, Virginia, a young artist has offered to draw his portrait. Nathan had, of course, refused, but then a thought had hit him...

He held the picture up to the tavern owner. "Is there any chance you've seen this man? He's a paramedic... or some type of medical personnel."

The man took the sketched portrait with a slight scowl, then his eyes suddenly widened as they fixed upon the tattoo of a crown of thorns on the man's neck. He met eyes with Nathan, a mixture of curiosity and suspicion.

"Why are you looking for this man, son?"

"He helped me... one time when I was really in need. I want to... I want to return the favor."

The owner's eyes again looked down. "Son, I've never seen the man myself. But there's a woman in this town named Maggie—been a troubled girl for as long as I could remember, and as a last-ditch effort, her grandmother, an old-timer who's been here her entire life, took her in. Well, it didn't seem like things were working out, and one night the girl tried to take her own life—cutting her wrists and hiding out in the barn. Well, she claimed a man who said he was a medic showed up, spoke to her, then brought her to Doc Hollison's place here. When the doc checked her out, he claimed Maggie's cuts were already a week into healing."

Nathan gave an uncomfortable smile. "Kind of freaky, isn't it?"

"That's not the half of it, son. When Maggie described the man in church—" the tavern owner stopped short. "Excuse me, at our town meeting that week—speaking of his strange tattoo of a crown of thorns on his neck, Winston Batten—a Brit who moved here about a dozen years ago, turned as white as a ghost. He'd fought in the Islamic Revolution years back. Claimed he was mortally wounded on the battlefield, reciting what he was sure to be his final Rosary, when a medic came out of nowhere and somehow patched him up. Winston said he could feel bullets zipping by as this man carried him through the center of the battlefield—unscathed—until they reached an allied medical facility."

They stood there momentarily, looking at each other as two who had no idea where to take the conversation at this point. By now, Nathan was no longer caught off-guard by the revelations. He had discovered at least one person with a similar story at each town in which he had played. Sometimes it was not until after his gig that a person would come forward. But he had yet to turn up a goose egg on this quest.

"Any chance," he began, "I could speak to these two people?"

The man shrugged, still not knowing what to make of the entire situation. "Son, I'm a believer, and I'll admit, I don't always understand the ways of the Almighty. I do believe He looks after His own, though. You want to be chasing an angel, that's you're business. I just hope you're open to what you might find."

iv

Annie D. put the last item in her shopping cart—an old-style top for the boy, Felipe—then placed her hand on the reader as she moved towards the door. As she was essentially the only member of their small contingent that was *not* avoiding the government authorities, it was left to her to engage in any purchasing required. Though she despised the concept of receiving the monthly government check, she was grateful, at least in their current circumstances, that she could provide the necessities for the few of them on her sole "income."

She wheeled her cart out onto Main Street in what was referred to by the locals as *The Village*, then turned to head towards the supposedly abandoned St. Louis Parish.

"*Zdravstvuj*, Annie."

Her head snapped up, turning from one side to the other.

That was Russian!

But she could see no one. "Who's talkin', if you please?" she demanded.

But there was no answer. She shook her head and again began to push the cart, this time at a rate that made it clear she was in no mood to linger. A shiver went down her spine as the hair on the back of her neck stood up.

She stopped, instinctively, and turned. There, standing in the center of the intersection, stood a very pale Vladimir Ivankov, her deceased husband's old boss, without a trace of emotion on his face.

A car was speeding towards the intersection, and Annie was unable to prevent the scream from emerging from her mouth. "Vlad! Look out!"

But the car did not hesitate. It passed right through the phantom, who still remained motionless, only staring intently at Annie.

"I'm not knowin' if yer friend or foe," she whispered. "But I'll have you know, I'm not woman without defenses."

She pulled out her Rosary, closed her eyes, and no sooner had she made the sign of the cross than she opened them, and the image was gone.

"I see that I'm owin' you one, My Lady." Annie breathed, then turned around, continuing her prayer as she went.

20

I have no pleasure in any man who despises music.
It is no invention of ours; it is a gift of God. I place
it next to theology. Satan hates music; he knows
how it drives the evil spirit out of us.

– Martin Luther

i

"If we could dispense with the pleasantries and just get to the matter at hand, I believe that would be best. Your absence at the emergency G.C. Council meeting was irritating, but in the end, perhaps it served its own purpose."

Anaxagoras, a.k.a. 'The 12th Imam'', struggled as best as he could not to make his trembling before the Mystic King evident. Yet the quivering of his voice betrayed his desires.

"Y-Yes, my lord."

Jimi T. nodded in acknowledgement and leaned back in his seat behind the intricately crafted desk. He clearly savored living in his Vatican quarters... at least the irony of dwelling on who had lived there before.

"You have defied me, perhaps even conspired with others against me, Anaxagoras. That is regrettable. But the truth be known, I have little time for this. Had it gotten out publicly, I would have had no choice but to make an example of you. But fortunately, with the assistance of our good Brother Siro, that has not happened."

Anaxagoras found himself confused. Was this the way of the Anointed?

"I-I do not understand, my lord. What is it that will become of me?"

Jimi T. looked confused himself. "What do you mean?"

"Am I... am I to—"

But Jimi T. waved him off. "Listen, Anaxagoras. I understand that many of my actions have been... *perplexing* to you, and perhaps others. I do not expect you to understand. But I need you, and I need the Council. I cannot do this on my own. We have an opportunity here that is even greater than we had originally imagined."

"But... if I may... your actions seem to be giving hope—"

"Not hope, at least not in the way the *Cortät* might understand it. I am bringing order. Our Master is less concerned with *what* he is sovereign over, so long as it is *he* that is sovereign. You must open your mind to the spirit of possibilities!"

Anaxagoras did not immediately respond, yet there was definitely something here that he found alluring.

Jimi T. got up from his desk and came around to where Anaxagoras was seated. He instinctively stood, as the Mystic King placed his hands upon his shoulders, looking directly into his eyes via the dark sunglasses.

"You must trust me. I need the confidence of the entire Council. A kingdom divided against itself will fall."

With that, Jimi T. dropped his hands and moved casually back to his seat behind the desk. Anaxagoras remained standing, clearly baffled by both the words and gestures of the Mystic King. Jimi T. continued.

"I do thank you for your time, and your consistent work for the cause. You are dismissed."

Anaxagoras blinked. "My lord, I am free to go?"

Jimi T., who had already started to look through other papers on his desk, looked up.

"Yes, you are."

"That is it?"

The Mystic King paused for a moment, deep in thought, then leaned back in his chair.

"Well, perhaps there is one other matter we need to address..."

DOMINION

ii

"What do you mean you have never heard of him? He worked here, he gave me his card!"

"I am sorry, sir, but I am telling you, we have no record of a paramedic named Ralph Tobit."

Nathan was exasperated. This was the end of the line for him. "I don't think you can completely appreciate what I've done to find this man over the past ten months. I've walked from one end of the country to the other, looking for him. And you know what?"

The medical receptionist who had offered to assist him looked back at him blankly.

"Every town, *every one*, had at least one person who had been helped by a paramedic with this description. I can't quite put it together, but some claimed it was as long as thirty years ago. In some towns, I thought I'd finally turned up a goose egg, but after I played the gig, people seemed to come right out of the woodwork to tell me he had been there at a particularly critical time in their lives."

The woman nodded sympathetically. "I really don't know what to say to that, sir. I've even entered his name into the national database as well. There is no licensed medical person with that name. Perhaps if you let me look at his card, I can—"

Nathan shook his head in frustration. He was feeling the anxiety waves start to emerge again. "I don't have it… a friend tore it up."

"I see…"

"How about this. Do you have a record of medical personnel coming to my house?"

"Certainly, just place your hand on the scanner and lean forward for the optical reading."

Nathan hesitated. "I-I'm afraid I can't do that."

"Sir?"

"Listen, it's really complicated, but I don't want certain people tracking me."

She looked at him for only a moment, glanced briefly down at his hand,

and then spoke in a quieter tone. "The address?"

"1313 Dolorosa Way."

She touched the screen a few more times. "Well, I see we've been out there a number of times. It appears the person we saw there, Nathaniel Freeman-Page, is deceased."

What?

"It's been a bad few years, but I can assure you, I am quite alive."

The woman again looked at him, this time with an expression that he could not discern as being suspicion or just curiosity. If she recognized the name, she certainly did not show it. Nathan noted the locket at the end of her necklace, which had fallen unclasped, revealing a picture of an infant girl.

"Cute kid," he mused absently.

The receptionist tried to maintain her composure as she clasped the locket shut, but it was clear that she was momentarily unsettled.

"Thank you, Mr. Freeman." She spoke quietly, just above a whisper, then returned to the task at hand. "If you can remember the date, perhaps?"

"The date?"

"When the paramedic came to your home?"

"Oh... jeez... it's been what... about five years now? Does that narrow it down?"

The receptionist nodded, touching her screen a few more times. "That leaves me with three possibilities."

Nathan thought for a minute, then a memory struck him. "His assistant... the guy had a really strange name..."

She touched her screen again. "Szandor Pike?"

"Yes! That's it! So what was his partner's name?"

But the receptionist only shook her head. "I'm sorry, it shows that Mr. Pike was there alone."

"Alone? No, that's crazy! He was there with the guy called Ralph!"

"I'm sorry, Mr. Freeman, but this is what the report states."

"Do you ever send paramedics out by themselves?"

She looked at him inquisitively. "Well, actually, I have never heard of that happening." She looked back at the screen. "This is interesting because Mr. Pike doesn't have the proper credentials to be out without a lead paramedic. Nonetheless, that is what the report states."

Nathan dropped his elbows onto the raised counter and lifted his hands to his head, grasping at his stubbles of hair. Even the confusion in his life was getting convoluted. He needed to talk to someone, and today was the day when he believed he might be at his final destination for solving the riddle of the paramedic who had paid him a kindness. A thought suddenly struck him.

"Hey, can you give me the address of the Szandor guy?"

"Mr. Freeman, you know I can't release—"

"Well then please, you can contact him yourself, just ask him—"

"Ohh…"

The woman suddenly looked ashen.

"What is it?"

"I am afraid that Mr. Pike is deceased."

"He's dead?"

She touched her screen a few more times, and then a look of understanding came across her face. She looked back to Nathan, somewhat unsettled herself from this process.

"Mr. Pike was a casualty of… ahh… the incident that took place three years ago."

"You mean the 'Great Deception'?"

She spoke, suddenly even more guarded. "I suppose… if that is what you want to believe it was. He, along with eight hundred million others across the globe, are clearly not being deceived anymore."

At this point, Nathan eyed the woman suspiciously. As he stared at her, his eye was caught by the brown cord slightly protruding from her shirt. He knew by this time what it was.

"You're scapular is showing, you'd better be careful."

The receptionist looked down anxiously and buried it under her shirt.

"Thank you, Mr. Freeman." She hesitated a moment, then spoke again. "I realize that I haven't been much help in finding your friend. But perhaps I can be of assistance to you?" She reached out her hand. "My name is Chloe,

Chloe Ostan—" her eyes suddenly widened, as she corrected herself. "Miller... Chloe Miller."

"You're having problems with your own name?"

She smiled sheepishly. "I'm sorry... I... I guess using my maiden name is a hard habit to break."

iii

The young girl screamed out in agony as Enoch attempted to restrain her on the hospital bed. He wiped her forehead with a wet cloth while the doctor continued to work on her abdominal area.

He looked down to the doctor, who looked back and shook his head. Enoch lowered his head in dejection as the girl's breathing slowed until it reached a leveling point, and she fell unconscious.

He released his grip and stood, looking back to the doctor, whose nurse was now attending to the woman. The doctor stood himself, removed his mask, and sighed.

"She lost the baby?" Enoch inquired, already knowing the answer.

"Yes," he responded. "It was all I could do to save her life." The doctor hesitated, looking carefully at Enoch before speaking again. "I don't know exactly how to bring this up... but... well, some say that you are a prophet, returned from the days of old."

Enoch cocked an eyebrow as he seated himself in a chair nearby, not quite interested in the current topic. "Do they?"

The doctor nodded, and gaining some courage moved towards Enoch, sitting down on the seat across from him.

"Yes, they do. Some even say you are Enoch returned from the bowels of the Earth, which confuses me, as I also see that you call yourself Christian."

"I do."

The doctor continued to wrestle with his approach, seeing that this man had no interest in providing any information unsolicited. Still, he proceeded.

"It doesn't matter to me, really. I've been a Jew my whole life, and I always will be. But what does your Christ have to say about what is happening here now? Our scriptures say nothing of this, except that somehow history is repeating itself."

The doctor searched Enoch's face up and down for some sort of a response but received none. Enoch just continued to sit and look down at the girl. Not willing to let it go, the doctor persisted.

"This girl was the last in all the surrounding villages that was with child. I have heard of no births in over six months in all of Israel, and know of no other pregnancies. And, and the boys…"

The doctor suddenly looked as if he were about to choke up. "M-My son Abel… he was my first… and now he is gone, like all the other firstborn males for as far across our nation as I have heard. What in the name of God is happening to us?"

Enoch raised his head and looked with sad compassion upon the man who was so desperately trying to make sense of what was transpiring in his little nation of such great history.

"What you have seen here is not in God's name. This is the Great Tribulation, of that I am sure. Only, it seems something has gone wrong. I do not pretend to know the ways of *Elohim*, but I tell you that something has gone terribly wrong. It was not to have been this way…"

21

In my frailness

    I am

    that which I despise.

.........betweer. the garden and the pit

......between the shadow and the spark

...between the impulse and the twitch

Lays the vine.

A seed

Not of the light,

    ...but its darker twin

Has set root within me

    tearing at my very innards

    holding tightly

        to the final sprout of wheat

???   ???   ???

    so fragile

      so starved

        so desiring

    to be made Whole.

The thorn has pricked the rose...

Can one not see?

    My heart's justice is swift

      ...and brutal

DOMINION

Can a sheep not choose to be lost
        to a shepherd
        no longer worthy
        of his given flock?

The wounded shepherd laments
        ...begging for exculpation
        from this malicious charge

"Release Me", he cries
        Accept me, he dreams
                des *froY* me, he prays

The sheep...
        ...the shepherd
The wheat...
        ...the tares
The pain...
        ...the love...

                Are One.

                – Jonathan Corban Storm
                    Unforgiven

i

"I do not understand, I have done exactly as you have instructed," the newly elected Prime Minister of Israel, Avera Kaifess, pleaded. "But still, our women no longer bear children, and our son's... our firstborn, have all died."

The Mystic King folded his hands pensively and leaned backwards. "It is obvious that the Spirit of the *Kôles* is still displeased with your people, Prime Minister."

Kaifess looked desperately perplexed. "But how can this be? We have not interfered with the natural progression of your religion. We—"

"Oh, my dear Kaifess, but you have."

She stopped speaking and looked upon the Mystic King, awaiting enlightenment. "How, my lord?"

"Your people continue to hide and protect the *Dishalåk*... the greatest threat to the world's spiritual peace. For this, the Spirit has reigned down punishment upon you."

Kaifess thought momentarily, then spoke. "Of this fact, I have been unaware. One has been banished from our nation, under punishment of death. But... if these two men are captured and turned over to your custody, the curse upon our nation—our people—will then be lifted?"

The Mystic King nodded slowly. "Yes, Kaifess, of that, I promise you."

Kaifess leaned back and released a relieved sigh. "Oh, thank you, my lord. May your days as sovereign be long. We will apprehend these enemies of the state. I will see to it myself."

"Very good, Kaifess. But there is one more, small matter."

"Yes, my lord?"

"I understand that the Great Temple is nearing completion, years ahead of schedule."

"Oh yes, my lord. I spoke with our master mason, Hiram Tyre, yesterday. The favor of God has been instilled in these workers, and they have proceeded with the Wisdom of Solomon and the strength of Samson."

The slight smile emerged from Jimi T.'s face. "I am sure. I speak to you of this, as I would ask the privilege of presiding over the re-dedication of the Temple."

Kaifess' mouth fell agape. "Oh, my lord, it would be an honor... the Great Protector of the Jewish Nation, presiding—it will no doubt be a most momentous event!"

ii

Nathan walked completely unmolested down the street in what was once the worst section of Harlem, thanks—at least in part, perhaps—to his newfound discovery that he was officially dead. His closely shaved head and meticulously trimmed beard, all bleached to a fine yellow-white, seemed to provide the additional cover he needed.

Does anyone even remember me anymore?

The receptionist known as Chloe, despite being unable to locate the mysterious paramedic named Ralph, graciously assisted him in securing discreet passage back to the east coast. He had met many intriguing individuals along the way in this curious network that seemed to be not unlike a modern day underground railroad.

Again, he was certain that these people were Christians, seeking perhaps nothing more than to live and let live. Yet despite his growing disillusionment with The Way of Mystic Realism, Nathan could not argue the point that the streets—and the world for that matter—were safer now because of the Mystic King and his following. Children were happily playing outside in the streets, teenagers were helping the elderly with their groceries, and there was just a general sense of contentment.

Still, in reflecting on his own situation, Nathan did not believe that the Mystic King would have fallen for this ruse of being dead. Publishing the work of Jonathan Storm—he was pretty certain now—would be seen as an act of direct defiance. And despite what was probably Siro's account of him "vanishing" in Norfolk after Kako had stuck him with some weapon, it was unlikely that this would be sufficient evidence for Jimi T. He had ways of *knowing* things, and Nathan was pretty sure that, at the moment, the Mystic King just had some bigger fish to fry.

The truth be known, despite the meticulously planned out passage Nathan had received at the hands of Chloe and her associates, he had felt as if he were being followed on several occasions. He also noted that he had not had a single vision or dream of Jesse or Mrs. Storm—or of anyone for that matter—for some time.

If I ever did have them in the first place, he thought to himself.

He was on his way to the train station now, having decided to lay low in a town outside Bangor, Maine—a location Simon had told him his uncle obtained years back to hide out when the "Feds" got too powerful.

Simon.

He had not thought of him for some time. But at this point, not much really mattered anyway, did it? Nathan had gotten all he needed from the world and was now ready to quietly back out, and live a long, restful life without any religion, politics, or other complications. Just him and his guitar.

As he walked, he became aware of a familiar sound. It was music... the music of *The Phoenix*:

> *I feared I'd never leave this place alive*
> *What can't be cured can still be cleansed in fire*
> *You've stung my heart, but I'll never give my soul*
> *But my passions may keep me forever near your hold...*

It was *Personal Demon*. The last time he had heard that piece outside the studio was when he had tackled Joey Escario in that old has-been nightclub.

The music cut off, however, followed by some significant shouting. Nathan watched as several *Ræpōī* skirted down the street and into the building from which the music appeared to have originated.

Nathan nearly stopped to see this incident out, but then found his eye caught by some graffiti on the side of an old abandoned Baptist Church.

†

Jonathan Lives

His heart jumped, and suddenly he found himself sweating. A chill shot down his spine as he decided to pick up the pace to his destination.

iii

"You've received the transmission from the Witness?" Annie D. inquired.

Sawlus nodded her head solemnly.

"Then you'll be leavin' us?"

Again she nodded affirmatively.

"Aye, then," Annie D. began, trying to remain cheerful. "Go with the grace of God, pet. I may not even know your name, but you've been like a daughter to me since we've been together."

DOMINION

Sawlus moved over and embraced the mother-figure, each weeping lightly, and Sawlus could not help but wonder if she would see her, or any other members of the Christian Resistance, ever again.

22

The Signs of the Times

<<n 6.088>>

JERUSALEM, Israel — For the first time in nearly two millennia, the Jewish Temple has been rebuilt.

Despite Judaism being the last fully intact, formalized religion holding a belief in a God, the Mystic King has permitted the Jewish faith "to come full circle, completing its full cycle."

Jimi T. Expo has continually emphasized the debt which mankind owes the Hebrew people for providing a structure that led many of the *Čidentûl* back to the ways of the *Kôles*.

The Mystic King will serve as the Master of Ceremonies for the dedication of the new Temple, being held tomorrow before sundown.

i

The Spirit of the *Kôles* flowed furiously through the throng. Nearly ten million followers lined the pathway and beyond to witness their Mystic King passing through their midst as he made the momentous trek to the Jewish Temple.

Sawlus hid amongst the crowd, a hood covering most of her head and face. She had no doubt that, if recognized, this crowd would rip her limb from limb. Though she could not see them, she knew Elijah and Enoch were also hiding somewhere amongst the horde. She kept this thought in mind in an attempt to provide her spirit some consolation as waves of anxiety intermittently swept through her.

As the crowd's cheers grew louder, she turned to see the procession approaching on foot. Sawlus could quickly discern Jimi T. Expo, the so-called Mystic King, who was adorned in all black with a heavy cape, and his usual dark old-style sunglasses. His notorious subtle smile rested on his face.

On his left ambled the aged Rabbi Solomon Abrams, his expression was one of enthusiasm, perhaps mitigated by just a twinge of sad nostalgia. Three meters behind were a very subdued Caliph Ali Bakr and none other than the Great Prophet, Tæsír Hoc, who peculiarly did not seem to particularly care for the event all that much. Siro Scribner, Sawlus' Þreha of many years, was another five meters behind wearing a bright grin and fervently waving to the supporters.

As the procession grew closer, Sawlus' eye was caught by something else about Jimi T. It seemed that his right arm was extended a little, as if he might be carrying something. She stepped, carefully, through a few more people in the crowd in order to discern what she was seeing. She moved forth until she was only two rows behind the front of the crowd and saw...

Caleb.

It was her son, now at the threshold of pre-adolescence, walking with the procession, Jimi T.'s arm slung around his shoulders. Caleb smiled brightly, and he would periodically look up affectionately at Jimi T., who would return a proud glance.

Sawlus' felt as if she had been stricken momentarily by overwhelming nausea. She had been sure that Caleb would be here. She had no doubt that he had been beguiled under the Mystic King's spell, but seeing the two of them together like this was almost more than she could bear.

She wanted to cry out, and found herself for the first time grateful that her vocal cords refused to heed to her wish. She would have to be strong.

The man moved stealthily through the crowd. He had waited a long time for the moment that was about to take place. He had been clean for a solid week, a feat which he had not accomplished in God knew how long. What's

more, his lame hand had even twitched a few hours earlier—he was sure of it—
and the delirium tremens had, for the most part, ended that morning.

For the first time, and perhaps the last, he was focused on his purpose
in life.

The crowd continued to cheer and chant as the procession came within
a hundred meters of the Temple. Sawlus sensed the misdirected joy circulating
throughout the scene as her son and archenemy approached her.

When they were no further than ten meters away, a glint of light caught
Sawlus' eye from the crowd lined along the opposite side of the cordoned off
lane. No one else apparently noticed as a man stepped out into the path of the
procession. In what seemed like slow motion, the man pulled an automatic
weapon out from beneath his coat. Recognition hit Sawlus like an express train.
It was then that all threads of reality seemed to fall apart.

SIMON! she screamed in her mind.

Only it did not seem to ring out only in her thoughts. The crowd grew
eerily silent as a suddenly distracted Simon Wilson looked to her, a perplexed
expression on his face. His eyes narrowed momentarily, and then a slightly
confused look of recognition hit him. He pursed his lips to call out her name
when a different voice cut through the surreal scene.

"Mother?"

Sawlus jerked her head around and saw her child, along with the
remainder of the crowd, staring at her blankly. She looked back in terror as she
saw one of Jimi T.'s bodyguards draw his pistol, aiming at Simon.

The crack of the gun was not enough to break the spell that seemed to
blanket the scene. Sawlus saw Simon's body jerk backwards as he fell to the
ground. Bright red fluid emerged from the shoulder of his left arm, and his
weapon slid from his fingers. He lay there, momentarily stunned, but the look
of determination on his face would not heed.

It would not end this way.

All time stopped. His left arm—and what he had come to call his *good*
hand—would not respond. Simon, dripping with sweat and blood, looked up to
the blistering sun. Pictures of a lifetime that seemed perhaps a million years ago
flashed in his head. He turned his gaze downward, staring at his right hand.
Simon closed his eyes momentarily, and felt a surge of energy shoot through his
body. His right hand twitched, then suddenly, astoundingly, closed into a fist.

This right hand, lame for what seemed to be an eternity, reached over and grasped the weapon from where it lay at his side.

Sawlus' eyes shot back to the procession, only perhaps ten meters from Simon, and saw that they had frozen in their footsteps. Both Jimi T. and Siro stared back at her, perhaps for the first time in Jimi T.'s case, unsurely. The bodyguard seemed to be struggling with his weapon, which had apparently jammed, as Caleb took one merciful step in the direction of his mother.

A series of shots rang out, and Sawlus saw that Simon had regained his focus to continue with his mission. She looked on as the body of the Mystic King jerked once... twice... three times in a sickening fashion. All those around him dove to the sides, except for Caleb, who stood dumbstruck between his mother and the man he had come to know as his "Abba". Sawlus could do nothing but look on in terror.

Finally, a shot struck Jimi T. Expo's head, blowing the left side of his skull completely off. He crumbled to the ground as the remainder of the crowd broke from the peculiar spell and plunged onto the assassin.

Sawlus tried to get to her son but was knocked to the ground by the mob running crossways, looking to get just one small piece of this most unholy assailant.

Caleb knelt at Jimi T.'s side, weeping bitterly. He lifted what was left of Jimi T.'s head and pressed it against his body, trying in a futile fashion to stop the bleeding.

"No, Abba! No! Don't die... please *don't die!*"

He looked down helplessly. Jimi T.'s left eye was gone, along with the majority of that side of his head. The right eye, exposed to the known world for perhaps the first time, filled with blood, searched momentarily, then fixed on Caleb.

"My son..." he whispered.

"Yes, Abba," Caleb wept. "Tell me what to do, I—"

"There is nothing you can do, my son, except be true to me."

Caleb looked down at Jimi T., the tears streaming relentlessly down his cheeks. The eye glowed a pinkish hue, remaining fixed upon Caleb, as the Mystic King spoke his last words.

"I love you, my son..."

ASCENSION

"I love you too, Abba…"

And with that, Jimi T. Expo opened his mouth, was about to cough, but instead broke into a gentle giggle; then breathing his last, the Mystic King finally yielded up his spirit.

Amidst the commotion, two sets of hands grabbed each of Caleb's arms and pulled him, screaming, from the now motionless Mystic King's side. Though Sawlus had been knocked to the ground and nearly trampled to death, she breathed a silent prayer of gratitude as she saw Elijah and Enoch pull her son away from the monster who had possessed his soul.

23

In the history of mankind, there have been two instances where a man has been born completely cut off from the *Kôles*. These men were well documented in the Ancient Hebrew Scriptures, known as Enoch and Elijah, and are the *Ďishalák*.

Though not part of the *Kôles*, or Life-force Pool, the *Ďishalák* discovered a means to drain the Pool of Her energy, and manipulate Her for their own purposes. They in turn seduced the masses, beginning the diabolical process of infiltrating the *Kôles* with a type of psychic sewage. Over the generations, this pollution in the Life-force Pool began severely blocking many human's connection to the *Kôles*, cutting Her members off from each other. Millions have been born since, not disengaged, but almost fully blocked. They are those who feed into the worldliness of this existence, those who will refuse to relinquish the archaic concept of a god. It was not deemed righteous by the *Kôles*, to hate them, but to pity them. But all is not lost. Their partial blockage can be cleared through the proper use of the *Kôles* and the collective efforts of the Saved.

Through this manipulation of the supernatural Life-force, the *Ďishalák* have committed the greatest crime of humankind's existence; the denial of each soul's full access to the *Kôles*. The two have seemingly become immortal, and still live among us today. But their time, as is true with the Physical Entity, is limited.

Masteen:1-14
Book of Given Truths

ASCENSION

i

Nathan sat, still feeling numb, in the living room of his cottage on Frenchmen's Bay in the Acadia region of Maine. He was now without the luxury of his holovision, as he had thrown the unit out into the ocean nine days prior following the assassination of the Mystic King.

At that point, he had decided to cut all ties with the outside world. There was no longer anything there for him. He was about to pour himself another brandy-tea concoction when...

There was a knock at the door.

He jumped up from the sofa on which he lay, staring at the door. He was a half-dozen kilometers from the nearest inhabited house. Nathan momentarily convinced himself that he would not answer the door, but somehow, a compulsion brought him up to it and his hand was now resting on the knob.

The knock came again, and Nathan yanked the door open to see...

A woman from his life years ago, grasping tightly to the hand of a boy of perhaps ten or eleven years of age.

"My God," he whispered. "Paula..."

She smiled sadly as a tear slid down her cheek. She opened her mouth to speak her first words in three years.

"H-Hello, Nathan."

He was dumbfounded, still staring at her. He then allowed his gaze to drop to the boy, who seemed to be near comatose.

"Who... who is the boy?"

Paula bit her lip, smiled, and lost Nathan's gaze temporarily. She looked down to the boy as several more tears emerged, and then back at Nathan.

"This is your son... Caleb."

DOMINION

ii

Kako Edgar sat alone at a table amongst the small but still dense crowd at Chef Volo's Italian Restaurant in Atlantic City. Though the outside of the building was bare, the inside was adorned with holly, ornaments, and blinking lights, a not-so-subtle reminder that today was the once much-celebrated Christmas Day.

However, Kako was in anything but a festive mood. Since losing his *Þreha* more than four years before, everything in his life had become one huge drag. His accidental termination of the life of Nathaniel Freeman-Page resulted in a swift termination of his own—from employment with *The Signs of the Times*. It also earned him the hatred of millions of once-adoring fans of the erratic lead guitarist of Jimi T's mystical band.

Well, we all make mistakes, he mused, in his own self-indulgent sarcasm.

Yet today, Kako sensed something would be different. A cryptic message left on his desk that morning stated that someone had new information on his beloved, and to meet them here at this time.

What could possibly be new? Has she returned to this plane?

As he continued to lament his situation, Kako suddenly noticed that many groups were getting up from their tables, staggered by only a minute or two, and filtering out the front door. A few moments later, Kako experienced an eerie sensation as the last patrons exited the restaurant.

What the...?

He accidentally knocked his spoon onto the floor. He reached down to pick it up, and nearly jumped when now sitting across the table from him was a large man who looked peculiarly familiar.

"Hello, Mr. Edgar," his voice was clearly Russian. "It has been a long time since the first and last time we met. Do you recall who I am?"

It only took an instant for recognition to hit Kako. His heart rate accelerated as his stomach dropped, and he looked solemnly to the ground. "M-Mr. Gavrilenkov."

Andrey smiled. "Yes, I see your memory is not so bad. Let us see how well you can retain these three facts that I would like to share with you at this time. Fact number one: there is no one on this Earth whom I loved more than my dear daughter, Sascha Luneska. She was my main reason for living. Fact number two... are you getting this, Mr. Edgar?"

Kako nodded as he felt a light layer of cold sweat cover his body.

"Very good. Again, fact number two: I not only hold you responsible for taking my daughter from me and getting her messed up in that sick religion, but I hold you responsible for her death. Do you know, Mr. Edgar, that it was six months after she died that I learned of her passing?"

Kako met Andrey's eyes only for a moment, then looked down again. Yes, his exceptional investigative techniques had also made him a master at how *not* to be found, and it was the only way that he and Sascha had been able to elude her father for so long.

"I am not sure of your response, but nonetheless, fact number three: you will be lying on the floor of the restaurant with a bullet in your head within the next two minutes. Of that, I am certain, Mr. Edgar. And the truth is, my only regret is that I can only kill you once."

Kako did not immediately respond and glanced up for only a moment as Andrey Gavrilenkov pulled an old-style pistol from below the table, pointing it at him. Kako looked down, closed his eyes, and breathed what he thought would be his last words...

"She left me..."

Andrey was caught off-guard. "What? What did you say?"

Kako looked up as tears started to flow from his eyes. "She'd left me. That morning. I've never told anybody... there was no reason for them to know."

"What are you talking about? Left you? Why would she—?"

"She was pregnant," Kako choked out. "We found out while we were on vacation in Los Angeles. We were so excited, then something happened that night... as we slept."

Andrey was beginning to feel sick to his stomach as his insides began to churn. "Of what are you speaking? What happened?"

Kako shook his head as the tears continued to fall. "I-I don't know... not exactly anyway. She was gone when I woke up, and I called her on her iBerry. She told me she'd had a dream... and a dark man with green eyes had asked her if she wished to raise her child in the light or in the darkness. He showed her things... and when she awoke, she knew that she would be returning to her faith... the faith of her family, she said."

Andrey felt his own throat begin to constrict as he fought back the tears which desired to well up in his eyes. "You are... you are—"

But Kako would not relent. He had nothing to lose at this point. "I told her to stop speaking nonsense, it was just a dream, and to come back to me. She refused. She knew of my skills for tracking people, so I know that is why she disabled the *i-Nav* system. She was the cause of that horrible accident... and they say she lived for several minutes after being thrown from the car."

Andrey could not restrain his emotions, and his own tears began to escape from their ducts. His entire hand, still holding the pistol, began to quiver.

"I know you loved her, Mr. Gavrilenkov, but I loved her too. That day, I lost Sascha, our baby, and just about any sense of caring what went on in this world. She told me on the phone it was over... she said she was going home to you."

And with that, Andrey Gavrilenkov dropped his pistol onto the table and cried out loudly as he buried his head in his hands. He wept, yet these tears were now not only of sadness, but in a real sense, of gratitude.

"Go..." he breathed in between sobs. Kako hesitated.

"I said go!"

Not wishing to test the man's patience a third time, Kako quickly stood and left the restaurant.

iii

Tæsír Hoc stood before the thousands who had piled into the Jewish Temple for its inaugural service. Sadly, it would be the final service for the man who had made its rebuilding possible. His tattered body had been placed in the Holy of Holies for the prescribed one hundred and fifty days, and the Temple had been subsequently sealed. Today, they would celebrate the *Récræ Tüm*.

At his right stood the aged Rabbi Solomon Abrams, High Priest of the Jewish Temple. On his left, serving in his role as Imam Emeritus, was Ali Bakr. A third man, unrecognizable due to the thin black veil that covered his face, stood aside the Rabbi. His attire suggested that in some form he represented those of the Christian religion who had accepted the truth, and embraced The Way of Mystic Realism.

ASCENSION

"We gather together today, Great Spirit, in the name of Jimi T. Expo, our Mystic King, whom You have called home."

Though its intent was to provide a festive atmosphere, massive wailing was heard throughout the Temple, and perhaps even throughout the entire world as the service was being transmitted to every holovision on the planet via satellite.

The Great Prophet continued on. "But as always, Great Spirit of the *Kôles*, we must move on to complete Your will. And as the Great Teacher of the Modern Age, I humbly accept the burden of your Anointed, now as my own, as the new—"

"*Samuel...*"

The Prophet choked on his last word as the eerie-voiced whisper descended upon the crowd. All looked around, including a now perspiring Tæsír Hoc, in search of the origin of the voice.

He tried to regain his composure and continued on. "Ahh... is that you, oh Mystic King...? Do you bring a message from the other side?"

"*No, Samuel...*" the voice echoed on. "*But I do offer a sacrifice from this side.*"

Tæsír Hoc's heart sank as he heard shuffling from behind him and suddenly experienced the simultaneous gasp of eight billion people from across the globe. He turned swiftly to see, now emerging from the Holy of Holies...

"*Did ye not believe, oh Samuel?*" The grotesquely formed Mystic King demanded as he took several slow steps towards his old associate. "*Did ye not think that I too could rebuild the temple?*"

An uncharacteristic broad smile emerged sickeningly from Jimi T.'s face, as he moved closer with some difficulty, shedding the shrouds which had enwrapped him.

"*What in hell's name do you think you are doing?*"

"I..."

And with that, there was a clap of thunder, and a flash of light emerged from the Mystic King's outstretched hand. Two bolts of lightning pierced the ceiling of the Temple, striking home, and the man known as Tæsír Hoc, or Luther, or Samuel Teilhard, exploded into a countless number of pieces, baptizing the entire congregation in blood and burning flesh. Jimi T. thrust forth his other arm and suddenly behind the altar, flanking Rabbi Solomon

Abrams, Ali Bakr, and the mysterious veil-covered man, stood seventeen luminescent figures as the prior threesome also began to glow. The Mystic King drew both hands back, and with a dispersing gesture, sent the luminescent figures into the endless abyss. Two remained momentarily, each providing a nod of acknowledgement towards the Anointed, then intensified in their luminescence before vanishing from the scene.

The Mystic King smiled widely as he shed the last shroud and stood at the backside of the altar, completely naked. Not a soul about the Earth moved as he opened his mouth to speak.

"With this sacrifice, I declare this Temple consecrated to the Great Architect of the Universe." he began, then giggled lightly to himself. "The final test has been completed so that I may now reveal to the world my true identity… all look upon me, and hail the Almighty God Incarnate, the Spirit of the *Kôles*, for *I am HE!*"

iv

"So what can I do for you, young man?"

"I wish to enlist for the Global Communion Peacekeeping Force, sir."

"You look very young."

"I am eighteen… yet wise beyond my years, sir."

General Nick Orieton chuckled. "I like your arrogance, kid."

"With all due respect, it is not arrogance if it is true, sir."

"And why do you wish to become a part of the G.C. forces? Do you realize you would have to renounce your national citizenship?"

"I have no citizenship, sir."

"Really? And are you a member of The Way? It is not required, mind you, but my experience has been that it has been quite an asset, especially for upward mobility in the services."

The young man held up his right hand, revealing the Seal.

"Very good, boy. How long have you been a member?"

"One day, sir."

Orieton was intrigued. "One day, I see. No need to think things through I suppose?"

"I want to make a difference in the world, sir."

"And do your parents approve of your decision?"

"My parents are dead, sir. I was only a child. They were killed by Catholic extremists."

"That is very tragic... and from that point on, you hated the *Cortat*?"

"No, sir, I was actually raised Catholic by my uncle."

"Then why the change of heart?"

"I want my life to have meaning... to have a purpose. I thought my uncle found this in his Christian religion, but in the end it was just a sham. He killed himself... he was weak, and his so-called faith failed him. The Mystic King—he clearly has power beyond this world. He is someone I can depend on... he is someone I can believe in."

"I see. I have to say, you look a bit familiar to me. Do I know you?"

"I don't believe so, sir."

"Very well then, I accept your application, young man. Your name, if you please?"

"Adam Moore, sir, and it is my honor to report for duty."

Citations

Chap	Reference
	Salar-A-azam, Abu Mohammed. *Waiting for the Reappearance.*
1	Eliot, Thomas Stearns. *The Hollow Men, Poems: 1909-1925*, T.S. Eliot, 1925.
2	Einstein, Albert (1879–1955).
6	Wordsworth, William. "The Power of Music", *Poems in Two Volumes.* 1807.
	Georgiou, Steven Demetre, aka "Cat Stevens", aka Islam, Yusuf. "Peace Train", *Teaser and the Firecat*, A & M Records / Island Records, 1971.
9	Menuhin, Yehudi (1916–1999).
18	Aristotle (384 B.C.–322 B.C.).
19	Nostradamus (1503–1566).
20	Luther, Martin (1483-1546).

For additional information on authors, artists, works, and quotes cited in *Dominion* (including the ability to purchase) please visit www.thedominionproject.com/citations.htm

The Dominion Project continues with Book VI

ABYSS

Altering Void

The sole and uncontested sovereign of the world, Jimi T. Expo, moves forward unfettered in his initiatives to bring order to an embattled but evolving civilization. Now in possession of fantastic abilities from his brief period outside of temporal existence, he seeks to quell all forces that would hinder his "divine" purpose. Annie D. Nesterov, aged in body but invigorated in spirit, leads a small resistance from within the confines of a "Purification Center", Mystic Realism's 'final solution' for those who still cling to their antiquated belief in a Christian deity. A still-conflicted Nathan, now serving in the role of protector of his family, tentatively tests the faith of his one-time friend, Jesse. But will this seemingly half-hearted commitment be sufficient to weather the inevitable storm of pain and suffering that gathers on the horizon?

Order your copy at

www.thedominionproject.com

Direct Ordering of the Dominion Series

Especially for those who do not have online access, all books can be purchased direct from T.C.C./Sacrata Dei Press by mail.

Dominion – The Series

Book I: Seed	*(June 2009)*
Book II: Phoenix	*(July 2009)*
Book III: Tryst	*(August 2009)*
Book VI: Requiem	*(October 2009)*
Book V: Ascension	*(December 2009)*
Book VI: Abyss	*(May 2010)*
Book VII: Revelation	*(January 2011)*

Dominion – Reference

For the Dominion reading enthusiast who wishes to delve deeper into the series, these brief reader's companions/reference are a helpful in that they provide character profiles, time and location references, summaries, background, and descriptions. Each Interlude is meant to follow its corresponding book from the series, offering a deeper understanding of the "Dominion world" while further preparing for the next book.

First Interlude
Second Interlude
Third Interlude
Fourth Interlude
Fifth Interlude
Sixth Interlude
Coda: Deux Ex Machina

Please call (574) 307-0413 for current mailing address, shipping rates, and tax rates (where applicable). Once obtained, please identify in your mailing your name and address, which book(s) you are ordering and the quantity, and provide a check or money order in U.S. dollars made payable to T.C.C./Sacrata Dei Press.

www.ingramcontent.com/pod-product-compliance
Lightning Source LLC
Chambersburg PA
CBHW031427250626
47155CB00004B/1649